They Don't Want us Here

By Kevin Watson

Foreword

This novel, *They Don't Want Us Here* is of racial and social significance. It is a shocking story of how a Housing Association faced with a blatant racist attack on one of its black tenants, even to the point of attempted arson, failed to apply its own tenancy agreements and housing policy to ensure his safety.

Although written using a fictitious mode of writing, the novel form, the story that unfolds is actually true, and happened to the author. It is for this reason that the book written and why its content comes over with such power and authority, rather than just being a product of imagination based on disinterested research, as happens in the case of most novels making social comment.

As a result this book is more than social comment. Because the book is rooted in reality and experience of its author, it stands out as a much more potent piece of literature, which ought to be read and understood by anyone brave enough to face what Britain still is, and what black people can still be forced to suffer in 21st Century Britain. From this view point, in these times of political correctness, it makes very challenging and uncomfortable reading.

The main argument of the novel is that faced with unreasonable behaviour on the part of two tenants, the Housing Association, failed to respond. Even when complaint was lodged the housing officer was completely out of his depth and constant calls for help using the help line were ignored. Even when the Association did respond the complaints machinery operated in such a way as to wear down the complainant by prevaricating and claiming lack of communication from the aggrieved tenant. The result was that the procedure never got above level one.

Further to this and what is more disturbing are the denials that came from the Association even when the person causing the problem was imprisoned for attempted arson. The behaviour of the police also according to this book was mixed. While they moved against the one tenant, after pointing out that the Association ought to have dealt with the problem, the Association did very little to support the police and when a complaint was made against the second tenant for committing a public order offence, against the black tenant. Nothing was done, and the Association faced with knowledge of the complaint insured that the new landlord knew about it as if the complaint was against the one complaining.

In the end the whole experience of attempted arson, and the deliberate noise made by the tenant who moved in later, put such a strain on the tenant that he ended up in a state of serious mental strain under the doctor. He also was prescribed medication that he would have to take for life.

The book shows that even with all this evidence in his favour the Association still denied any responsibility for the mental health of the central character in his bid to find some kind of justice. In short this is a work that spells out how the entire system failed at every level to provide duty of care and reneged upon its own tenancy agreement when tested at the basic level of tenant care and safety and its declaration that as an Association it moves swiftly against any kind of anti-social and racist behaviour. This is a book that not only ought to be read but should begin a serious social debate about the way such minorities are treated in the Housing Association system and in society in general.

K.J.Rosier

Chapter One

"I know it's not much of a view but the rent is cheap, and it has central heating," said the blonde woman; her hair tied in a ponytail, sporting fake suntan covering over her thick make up. She opened the door to the flat along with her companion another female. It looked big and had two bedrooms. I could not believe my luck. Here I was an unmarried man being offered a two bedroom maisonette flat in a lower middle class area. Wow!

"I see someone loves their booze around here," I said, noticing the dented cans of beer lying dormant around the bins.

"Oh... the council comes here every Thursday so that should not be a problem." They walked into the flat; it was adequate for a student I thought.

"So what are the neighbours like?"

"It's usually quiet around here. What are you studying?"

"I am studying music."

"Anyway here are the keys to the property," she said, dismissing my last answer.

"Wait until you see your new neighbour," she said with a roguish giggle, "she will love you...!"

"Why?" I asked, watching her turned into the small kitchen.

"She loves black men!" I didn't know how to take that last comment, but managed to forge a faint flickered of a smile, although thwarting.

"Unfortunately it is a prepaid meter; but you can have it changed if you want."

"That should be okay for a student on meagre means," I replied, looking around the pallid empty and spacious flat.

"I take it you don't know anyone around here?"

"No."

"Don't worry," she said almost with an aunt's sarcasm, "you will fit in around this part." She took out the tenancy agreement, and placed it on the clean kitchen surface ready for me to sign the papers. The kitchen was very small with only a small window, but at least it opened.

"Well you better sign your life away," she said, in a perceptive, and yet knowing voice of gloom.

Before long I was watching the women leaving, and jumping into the car, without even looking back, and driving off leaving trail of black smoke behind them. Walking into the flat I noticed how my footsteps were creating echoes around the empty place. The flat certainly needed carpeting... and a few bits that I didn't have at my old place I thought; looking around proud fully at my new home. I walked into each of the rooms.

"Wow I can't believe all this space is mine!" My watch showed 11:00am; when I heard the loud thumping music coming from the ceiling. That must have been the woman that had a thing for black men. Maybe she looked like Beyonce with firm big breasts, and alluring lips? Suppose she went around to my flat; asking for sugar as hers had ran out! Maybe she would wear her skimpiest satin night dress claiming that she had locked herself out of her flat and needed to crash on my settee? My curiosity got the better of me as all sorts of lewd thoughts raced through my inquisitive mind. I could hear the music pumping away, causing vicious vibration in my flat, but my curiosity only subdued what should have made me annoyed.

Anyway it was time that I did a bit of shopping, and started to fill this place up ready for September. I looked out the front window, and could see some white teenagers hanging around looking bored. They were probably around eighteen years old, probably younger; and wearing hooded outfit. Well it was the summer holidays, and most of the youth clubs were probably closed down, and they were all bored stiff.

Making sure that all the windows inside the flat was closed; I then locked my flat door and walked across the estate. I didn't have to walk far when I became aware that the white people in the area were eye balling my every movement. I felt like I was in the movie: "Wicker man," where everybody was a witch and I was to be their unwilling sacrifice. Maybe they hadn't seen a black man before, and didn't know how to approach us I wondered? Maybe if I was to offer the first piece of the olive branch their sour glares would soften?

"Morning," I said, offering a generous smile hoping that maybe it would be contagious. Black people were known to have the best smiles where we all walked around glaring our teeth to look less threatening. I had no reply just guarded dirt glares. This made me felt on edge; of being a strange alien of not belonging. At last I waited for the bus to take me into Wolverhampton town centre. I looked around the area noticing that I was the only black ball on a bright green coloured snooker table. There was a pale air of deadly silence almost written with a warning... by white ghostly fingers that this was a no go area for my kind. I could feel the tight tension, as athletes waiting for the gunfire to be fired forcing everyone to run quick off the mark.

It suddenly hit me ... from just a few miles down the road from where I lived, and already I had arrived in another world... of racial segregation.

There in Perton; the whites retreated into their own haven not wanting any aliens to upset their way of life, or even walking into their safe communities changing things. There were no black faces to be seen or Asians only one curry house; but the restaurant existed on white terms and for the benefit of white people. The stares reminded me of when I was a child, observing old Jamaican women with big hands built on slavery handling the fruit and vegetables with their unwashed shovels, only to place it back again after grumbling about the steep prices.

I felt handled, and picked like a discarded round black Spanish radish. With their eyes they hated me being there, I had dared to move into leafy Perton bringing with me my strange aroma of exotic difference.

Maybe they enjoy the Caribbean dark dishes served only feet away from the deep enticing ocean, from the black hands of the natives, but that was so different. They can taste the delights of the Caribbean getting drunk on good rum but it must not enter into Perton. But here I was walking into their culture; their closed space, uninvited maybe bringing with me a dish too hot for their consumption wanting to integrate? I was not as lucky as that Indian restaurant that enticed them with authentic balti dishes and golden coloured korma mixed with secret Indian herbs. They were okay.

The bus arrived, and I waited before getting on. After discussing the fair; I spotted a seat at the back. I worked my way through the white thick fog of frosty angry stare, assorted with suspicious looks; before taking my seat. It seemed like a long journey especially when the stares were thick like batter on fish.

"I wonder how long it will be, before they all arrive here!" An old lady snapped, quickly glancing behind her, showing tones of antipathy to her friend. It was an uncomfortable journey for me, not because of the bus driving over irregular bumps in the roads, which the Council under Labour had neglected, nor the summer sun shimmering through the grimy bus window; but the cold eyes letting me feel that I was a creature from outer space.

I got up, and departed from the bus outside the Wolverhampton art gallery.

It was not long before I noticed different colourful faces, a fusion of cultures, which just seem to come at me from every direction as a spaghetti junction intertwining or wind scattering through high trees. Just as I was about to search for odd bits I bumped into my black friend Darren walking up towards me. Darren was quite stocky having a rounded pleasurable face. His skin was soft brown.

"Hi Kevin"

"Hello Darren. I thought you would have been in Birmingham looking for girls! The weather is so hot and the legs are out... I know you're a leg man! God almighty this is booty summer this year!"

"Well I had to pop into college for a bit. They wrote to me saying that my music book was overdue. Anyway how is your place in Perton? You moved in today didn't you or was it yesterday?"

"It's a weird area!"

We slowly strolled towards the seats opposite the art gallery.

"What do you mean weird?"

"I don't know," I thoughtfully replied. "It's only 15 minutes drive from here, and yet it's like you're entering white rule South Africa. The hostile looks that I get is uncanny it's just unreal." We both sat down on the bench.

"Well last time this gorgeous shapely woman wiggled her butt past me; I went over to do some business only to see her rubbing up on another female. To me that's unreal!" Darren said, making us both laugh.

"What are your new neighbours like then?"

"I am glad you asked that question. The landlady told me that my neighbour will love me as she loves black men!"

"What! Let's go now what we're waiting for!" Laughed Darren. "Has she got Jennifer's Lopez butt? What does she look like? Has she got any sisters?"

"Cool it Darren," I said throwing up my arms signalling for him to calm down, "I don't know... I am just as curious as you are."

"Hey she could look like the elephant woman!" Darren laughed.

"You wish!"

"How old is this landlady of yours?"

"She's about in her thirties."

"What! Come on why would a landlady her age be telling you this? You would think that she would want your funky black ass for herself. It all sounds too fishy for me," said Darren laughing his head off.

I thought about this. Why would a white woman, up her own arse, thinking her job was too great; would want to pair me off with someone else without even flirting with me... whether she wanted me or not? Then again maybe Darren was just jealous?

"To be honest I am not sure whether I should have moved to Perton."

"Why? I was only kidding Kevin! Maybe your neighbour is related to the elephant man, but the genes could have missed her!" He said with a followed up wink.

"I might be paranoid; but when I took on the tenancy she more or less asked me to sign my life away as she handed me the documents. I didn't like that."

"Maybe she is just using a figurative speech that all don't take it too serious. You seem a bit tense Kevin," he said, grabbing my shoulders to massage them, "when was the last time you got laid?" We both laughed heartily.

"Look I'll check out this new place of yours sometime," Darren said standing up ready to go. "And try to get a piece of pussy you know reading too much of that bible of yours is not doing your chopper any good."

"Ha, very funny... not!"

After we touched fist together, we both went our separate ways. I worked my way down to Victoria Street until I arrived at the second hand furniture shop.

I opened the door, and was faced with quite a few settees and wardrobes in, but didn't like the look of some of the prices.

"Are you sure that these are furniture's are second hand prices?" I asked in disbelief. The grey haired woman who looked in her late fifties ignored my question.

"Have you just moved into a new place?" She asked in a harsh voice.

"Just today and I have nothing in the place yet." I laughed but, she barely broke a smile. "It looks as Jesus will have to skip turning water into wine, and throw down some furniture's from heaven at this rate for my flat." My comment seemed to make her eyebrow rise as she offers me one of her assiduous look.

I looked around the shop, looking at the prices; but then decided that the prices were outside my budget.

I turned towards the door when noticing a man struggling to carry some of the furniture's in.

"Do you want a hand mate?" I asked, much to the relief of the scruffily dressed man.

"Yeah there are quite a few chairs waiting to come in just pop them on the left of the shop."

I looked inside the van, parked on the double yellow line outside the shop, when noticing my work was cut out.

I never expected there to be so many chairs, and odd bits, but I had offered to help out. So I took off my jacket, and began the work.

"You don't find any good manners like this young man these days," said untidy elderly man. The shop assistant agreed, as she hands him some freshly made coffee.

"What a lovely cuppa," he said, watching me working away.

"It looks like we're in for a week of good sun, and I only forgotten to hand out some clothes on the line," the woman muttered.

"There's always tomorrow Dorothy. Here I tell you... did you hear the recent news of the recent stabbing in London?"

"I know isn't it outrageous? It makes you afraid to leave your own home," she replied with a shudder of the very thought of being attacked.

"Yeah... They want to bring back capital punishment or bring back the national service that will soon sort them all out. Since labour has come into powers they have done nothing for this country. They are running the country into the pits with their softly approach. Since they have been in power they've done nothing but lined their own pockets. It's an outrage!"

"They're all the same it doesn't matter who you vote in," she said.

"Look around Wolverhampton how many new businesses have opened up only to close down the same year. I tell you Dorothy... this government is killing the small business industry. And as for the bankers..."

An hour later I had just finished unloading the chairs and looked miserable for offering my help.

Now my day had been lost, and I had nothing to show for it, but watching the old man drinking, and talking about labour whiles I was doing all the hard work.

"Well all the chairs are in," I said, putting on my jacket and ready to leave.

"That's very kind of you young man. I wouldn't know what I'd do today without you," he said putting down his second cup of coffee.

"That's okay. I better be off."

"Wait there! What do you need in your flat?"

"What?"

I could not believe my stroke of luck.

"I need a wardrobe and a settee as I have moved into a bigger place, and a book shelf," I said slowly wondering what they were up too.

"Come with me young man," he said, walking slowly towards the back of the shop. "I will give you this wardrobe, and that leather settee, for £100 and I will also throw in the book shelf too. They have been hanging around here for six months now. I have no space for them."

"I couldn't do that to you. Look at them; they're Italian!"

"They should be... they came from a very wealthy couple who have packed up to go to New Zealand for their retirement.

They wanted to make sure that we sold it to the right person. It was sentimental for the couple you see. It didn't cost me a penny. You've earned it today as far as I am concerned."

"I will take it; I said in disbelief." I went to the till, and signed some papers still not believing my luck. That furniture's must have been worth at least five grand or more

"So what is your name young man?"

"Kevin."

"Well... I am Barry, and this is my wife Dorothy." He offered his hand.

"How do I arrange collection?"

"We'll deliver it for you the next day of you like?"

"Sounds fine. That's just great! Wow I can't believe it"

"Do you watch the news?"

"I try not to."

"What! A decent fellow like you?"

"Well it all the same recycled bits, and most of it is just about petty things like Gordon Brown is feeling miserable because he has lost a safe seat. What does he expect? I don't bother with politics," I said, hoping to leave.

"You're young yourself. What do you think is causing the knife crime that happening today amongst the youths?"

"That's simple question."

"Is it? Well no one else seem to know the answer!"

"It's all down to bad parenting. If you have a child brought up in a home that has no love... or little discipline, especially with no male role models then this is what you get... crime."

Barry encouraged by his discerning answer said, "I tell you young man during the second world war..."

"He doesn't want to hear it Barry," interrupted his wife knowing that he would go on forever.

"Are you a student?" He asked not pleased with his wife intercession.

"Yes I am I'm studying music."

"Oh I could never understand music. I can't even use a computer for that matter. My good wife she understands them a bit more than I do, don't your Dorothy?" She smiles encouragingly.

"England has gone to the dogs now Kevin. You have all the immigrants coming over... don't get me wrong you are born here you have a right to be here as anyone else who helped built this country but now England has become a country for freeloaders people who come here to scrounge off the state and abuse our system."

"I thoroughly agree with you Barry!"

"You do?"

"Of course I do! You could not go to some of these countries and get the kind of benefits that you get here so I understand where you are coming from."

Barry looked at me quite shocked. It was as if black people were not meant to be against an influx of immigrants coming into the country but somehow how be for it.

"No offence but I thought that most dark skin people would want more immigrants coming over here!"

"You will find that many of us are against it. It is hard enough competing against white people Barry," I said as we both saw the humour.

"Would you ever go back to where your parents come from?"

"No."

"Why not...? All that: sun, sea and sand?"

"Jamaican government since it became independent did not have a proper structure in place economically. Most of us would have loved to go back but to what?"

"So are you going away for the summer holidays Kevin?"

"I need to find work; but I am having no luck from the job agencies. On the telephone they tell me that they have jobs all lined up, and then I go in, and everything changes suddenly there is no work available..."

"Bah, you're coloured... that's what it is." He leisurely said, almost as if someone had offered to take him out bowling for the day.

"Pardon me?"

"It's because you're not white... that's why you're being mucked around. A nice fellow like you it's they loss."

"Well they don't think that Barry. It's getting really frustrating."

"You have to stay positive no matter what. That is why our business is still going strong we have survived labour's cruel hands. We will be selling up in two years, and off to New Zealand where we will retire leaving behind the rat race."

"Sound good to me Barry," I said.

"Look I need a hand twice a week getting in new stocks, as at my age it is getting too much for me running up and down those winding stairs, and into the van."

"Are you offering me work?" I asked. "Wow the lucky break I needed this is great!"

"I tell you what its cash too!"

*

I was on the bus waiting to arrive home. I thought on how my luck had changed that day. Here I was a student who had no luck in getting any summer jobs.

I would be envious to hear of how other students were in summer jobs that would eventually help financing their studies.

I also thought of the many employment agencies that I registered with, and how there seem to be no jobs going and yet my white friends would get work. I was not naive; I knew that racism played a big part to my disappointments, but to focus on it would not make anything better. I have known black men who had joined Islam because they were angry at what they regarded to be a white society which is infested in racial hatred. I did not want to become bitter. I tried to ignore that racism existed. Even if it was staring me in the face it didn't exist.

I had to be that role model for the black youths so that they could look up to someone who has made it in a white society that seemed maybe to undermine their achievement.

I also knew it was only through personal education that I could meet the challenges of a hostile racist Britain. These thoughts became a cushion for me against the uninvited cold stares. I jumped off the bus and walked past a different set of white youths all hanging around glaring at me. There were also I noticed more discarded beer cans outside the bins. Closing the door behind me, I locked it. It was almost symbolical I could shut out all the hate the horrible frowning faces and enter into his world being who he wanted to be.

In his world I didn't have to deal with racism, I was safe with the white friends who loved me. Where black, and white children; played together in the sand building sand castles against the deep blue calm sea.

I walked into the lounge invited not by Martin Luther King's speech of: 'I have a dream,' but the loud dance music thrashing against the wall.

This brought me down to earth with a sudden bang.

Here I was faced with loud music, by a shapely woman that, 'loves black men,' who I have never seen. What gorgeous woman who 'loves black men' would behave in this mad unsociable way? But there again am I wrong for suggesting that mad women can't be stunning? There must have been gorgeous women back in antiquity who were off their rockers?

I looked at the picture of my girlfriend for the first time; I then realised that she was as white as a sheet of winter's snow. I didn't notice this before; but now I noticed her Celtic subterranean soft emerald eyes. It was as if she was looking softly at me from the small passport picture. Why did I notice her white skin, and not before?

Maybe I was missing her, and longed to hold her in my arms and just sweep her away to some exotic location and ravish her?

There was a knock on my door, I looked out and was pleased to see a small firm that he had hired to move his odd bits from his old flat.

"Where do you want these buddy?" asked a round face man who looked as if he was not shy of drinking a couple of pints every night.

"Erm... Could you leave them in the lounge and I will sort it out later?" For the next 30 minutes they were moving in my belongings in followed by my cooker and then washing machine. My face brightened, now that my home was beginning to lose the echo and familiar items were seen around me. It looked like home. Now I could go to Church; I found one of the bags that my bible was in; everything was going to turn out just right. I had found work and my studies were bringing in good results what more could he asked for from life?"

Chapter Two

I woke up to loud music thumping though my wall I tried to bury my head under the pillow but it became too unbearable. I had to do something about it. Besides I had never met this woman before. I met some of the neighbours and they were not too happy seeing me around there so maybe she "loving black men" would at least make him feel welcomed. After slipping on my shirt and trousers I left the flat and knocked at her door.

"What do you want?" Shouted the woman from upstairs, sounding intoxicated and untutored.

"The noise is a bit loud and it is only 4am in the morning. Could you turn it down please?" She disappeared without saying a word. I returned to my flat and noticed the music had been turned down. I had never met her. But she certainly didn't sound like Pamela Anderson. Did she look like her at all? All kind of visions searched my inquisitive mind. Could she really have Jennifer's Lopez butt, being so intoxicating? When would she have the time to do some booty work out, if all she did was getting herself intoxicated? Somehow the picture didn't make any sense to me. I had to see her even if it was just to satisfy my curiosity. But then again there were girls at my college who were drop dead gorgeous, yet sounded as a wind up Barbie doll. There was still some hope yet for my mysterious neighbour.

I had to see this woman that the landlady said: "loved black men" Well it was too late for me to sleep now so I decided to go into the lounge area and watch some morning television.

It was now 9:00am and the music stopped ages ago. I got washed and dressed.

I got ready to leave my flat when I was approached by a white smiling white male with bristly face. He looked like he was going to sell me a second hand television or something just as dodgy. It looked as if soap had not touched his face in a few days.

"Have you just moved on the estate mate?"

"Yeah," I return my cynical tone wondering his next move. For all I knew he could have worked for Delboy in the sitcom: 'only fools and horses.'

"Have they told you about her upstairs?"

"No... not really; if you are referring to Bromford Housing Association. Why is there something that I should know about her?"

The strange man disappeared to lock his door, and then started to walk away from his flat. He looked like an impish bearded dwarf straight from Narnia.

"You have been the fourth person that has moved into that flat below," he whispered as if he was transmitting top secret information to me.

"What's so special about that? Do I get the Queen's telegram?"

"Forget the Queen's telegram! Neither of the tenants lasted two weeks!" My face dropped showing horror, now I stop walking away from him. My dream home maybe was not filled with pine trees and being the picturesque paradise after all. I should have known but I was blinded by what I thought was light at the end of the tunnel. Why would they have given a black man such a good flat in a white area?

There was always a catch somewhere even if at first it was not obvious but as spider that spins their web sooner or late it caught into the intricate deceit. There again maybe this stranger just wanted to drive me out before I settled in?

Maybe he didn't want black people living in his block? Maybe it was all reverse psychology in which to scare me out off my own home?

"How does she drive them out?" I asked still not trusting him or a word he had to say to me.

"She's nuts!" He spun his finger around his right temple indicating she's off her trolley. "She should be sectioned not here in Perton! She damaged my car because I wouldn't fuck her!"

I tried to take all this in. Was he playing games with me? Why was he telling me this? This did not make any sense to me. Was this the same woman that the landlady was saying loved black men? It just didn't add up. I was expecting some refined white goddess who spoke softly, and enticingly, not a thug. Maybe this neighbour of mine didn't have Jennifer's Lopez booty after all? Or why would he not sleep with her? Was my neighbour gay or something? Or maybe she was not his type? I had to set the record straight even though somehow I knew where the answer would lead me.

"What does she look like?" I blurted out as if I had to get it off my chest.

The stranger giggled and rubbed his face saying, "My God no horny prisoner escaping from wormwood scrubs would shag it; they would not get anywhere near it! She's that bad trust me! Wait until you see her; her breath stinks too!"

She's an 'it,' I thought to myself. Bromford Housing Association had moved me right beneath an 'It" I had to laugh to myself. I shook my head in disbelief and yet smiling.

"Do you want to share the joke?"

"It's nothing," I replied.

"Anyway I'm Scot."

"Nice to meet you Scot, I am Kevin."

Scot looks around to see who was listening, and finally over his shoulder.

"Look if you want anything on the side like DVD copies, music burns or computer just comes around and I will sort you out a good deal," he winks.

"I'm a computer scientist you see I know the computer inside out," he impishly sniggered.

"I better go to work."

"I can even get you computer or even music software!" I stopped walking, look behind me and then continued on my journey.

Later that evening I arrived home to rowdy music blaring at top volume. I was sure that the woman upstairs was loopy. I was about to sit down when I heard an angry woman shouting outside. Being one that liked to know what was going on; I went to investigate, but from the safe distant behind the window of his front door, only peeping through the blinds.

"Leave me a fucking alone... you wankers," She shouted out loudly which followed by her banging all the doors. My eyes darted around to see who she was shouting at then he realised that she was talking to herself! Suddenly it made sense to me. Now I knew what my landlady meant when she asked me to sign my soul away. There was something menacing about the place I had moved in. What was my neighbour capable of; apart from loud noise and screaming out of windows?

She obviously had mental issues, but surely it would not affect me or my living space? There was no Pamela Anderson or Jennifer Lopez butt; but an 'it'. She was scrawny, dirty and looked as if she had just risen from the grave. I went into the kitchen to fetch my tenancy agreement from on top of one of the cupboards. It warned about neighbours being a nuisance and creating noises. But how did she manage to drive out previous tenants; if the contract was enforceable in law? I could hear my girlfriend arriving; so I put back the tenancy contract. My girlfriend arrived letting herself in with a key that I had given her. We kissed. I missed her and it showed. I reached his arms around her trim waist. She had the most beautiful wavy auburn tresses that swept down her back as the river in Devon. Her sea green eyes were deeply Celtic her smile sensual and wide.

"I don't like the look of this place," I said, walking into the kitchen as she follows me.

"Do you mean that mad woman?"

"She's nuts!"

"I could hear her half way down the estate," Anne said.

"Do you know that I have never had a normal white neighbour yet living next door or above me? I actually thought that moving to Perton would change all of that!"

"What do you mean honey?" We both walked into the lounge holding our glass of squash.

"Well... my other white neighbour was a prostitute who was always rowing with her pimp; before her; it was a white man and he was dying from alcoholic abuse. Why can't I just get normal white neighbours; why do they have some kind of social dysfunction?"

Anne offered a sympathetic smile.

She didn't know how to reply to me. I didn't expect her to relate that would have been impossible. How could I relate to a blind or deaf person when my senses have not been taken away from me? I see the blue skies; the rippling lakes and rushing waterfall; that beauty I could not describe to someone who is blind or the sound to someone who was dead. It was just another word where the sound created that bridge.

"How has your day been a part from that noisy woman?"

"I came home from work hoping to have some peace but obviously that ruined my plan."

"Your friend Jonathon is coming around today isn't he?"

"Yes."

"He'll cheer you up even if I can't."

"Maybe he will..."

"Why don't you complain to Bromford and tell them that you have a very noisy neighbour above you?"

"I don't want to start making enemies Anne!"

"Do you really want her as a friend?"

"I suppose not."

"Well come on let's go on the computer and write a letter to Bromford Housing Association," she said switching on the machine that was in the corner of the lounge. As soon as we were about to work on the letter there was a knock on the door.

"That can't be Jonathon already?" Anne said, going to the front door but it was the woman from next door and she was intoxicated.

"Can I help you?"

"I want to apologise for the noise earlier on."

"Oh... that's okay. My boyfriend was a bit concerned he's a student and he like his peace and quiet."

"I was a student," she said.

"What were you studying?"

"Oh... Let me see... I can't remember! I don't want us to be enemies right?" She said, puffing up her flat chest, trying to look convincing even if it did look pathetic.

"Neither do we;" Anne said smiling sweetly.

"You don't have a fag do you? It's just like I'm so pissed if I get into me car I could get banned again!"

"No it's my last one. I don't smoke that often as I am trying to give up," Anne replied.

"Don't do that!" She shrieked, "I might want to nip around for a fag!"

I crept up to listen from behind the door to the two women.

"I have been here... seven years," she managed to say without falling over her.

"I bet you can't wait to move out," I said now walking towards the door.
She didn't like my comment.
"I'm Cynthia."
Anne introduced herself; but I didn't say anything. I remembered the warning from Scot.
"They have been trying to get rid of me for the last seven years," she said with a defiant tone, "And I am still here!" As she said those words Scot walked past when she reached out to grab him.
"I need some new dance music," she slurred her words.
"I'll talk to you later Kevin," Scot said, walking away with her. She disappeared into the next flat without even saying goodbye.
There she was one minute and the next she was gone.

"Thank God he came to the rescue!"
"I think she's quite nice," said a positive and naive dazzling- faced Anne.
"So is a rattle snake until you get up close to it!" And with those words I shut the door firmly. As far as I was concerned she could stay where she lived up stairs and not bother with my life.
"I suppose we don't need the letter now," Anne said, sitting down on the settee making herself more comfortable.

The evening past and we were in the lounge watching the BBC TV production of the great world war one with Jonathon.
Jonathon was a white man who had just entered retirement. But he was not taken it too good so he was often seen in the library from morning till late evening.
He would rather be anywhere but his home where he lived alone with his wide collection of his English and history books. At least in the library he could build castles in the air about being a student again getting up in the sunrise, and remaining there just to pass the time away. He didn't know that life after employment was so gloomy it was nothing to look forward too. He was a historian; his area of study, British history, so he was pro monarchy. He loved England with such a passion that it became his substitute for the wife and children often longed for.

"Oh its so tragic how many people have died during the war. What a tragic waste of human life," he tearfully said, as he watched the blooded bodies all strewn across the trenches.

"The Americans didn't join the war until we were literally on our knees... typical Yankees. It's only because the Germans were using the Mexicans to wage war with her, otherwise she would not have helped us!"

I didn't reply. I watched the archive footage dispassionately and the sentimental old fool.

"How come we knew that black soldiers fought in both the First World War and the second, and yet in the archives footage we only see white people?" I asked. There was an uncomfortable silence in the lounge.

"Anyone fancy coffee?" Anne interrupted

"Yes I will have one," said Jonathon, still glued to the documentary.

"Do you want one honey?"

"Yes please," I replied.

"You must be mistaking it for the Second World War, and they were only minor contribution," Jonathon said at last answered.

"Minor? I thought that the blacks fought the hardest, and were pushed to the front line to take most of the bullets," I challenged as I got up and went to the computer, logged onto the internet to do some research and prove my point.

"I'll look it up on the internet," I confidently challenged him.

Moments later; I excitedly said, "I told you blacks fought in both wars! What I don't understand is why in the BBC archives footage it is all white faces that is being shown dying and sprawled across the trenches?"

Jonathon turned away from the television in defeat and said, "The blacks could night fight side by side with the whites. They had to fight separately."

I could not believe what I had just heard. No wonder my white historian friend didn't really want to admit to black involvement in the war, I thought. I was listening to a white historian who was supposed to be my best friend who was willing to lie about history!

"What! Are you trying to tell me that the blacks who were laying down their lives for white people were still seen as inferior?"

"Yes," he replied now admitting to the truth.

"Well those blacks must have had a screw lose as I would have turned the guns around, and do some friendly firing inside my own trenches...ungrateful wretches!"

He was not amused by my comment. Anne returned with the cups of coffee.

"You are certainly moving up the world moving to this place," Jonathon said, after thanking Anne for the coffee.

"It's modest improvement."

"Is there a library around here?"

"Yes, a stone throw away," I replied.

"So in Perton you have Sainsbury, a library, you are doing well. One more step and you could end up in Buckingham Palace!" We both laughed easing the tension away from politics.

"So how are you taking your retirement, have you cracked up yet?" I asked him.

"No... I haven't just yet. I am dealing with my father who has dementia, and my mother who uses credit cards as if it is going out of fashion."

"Well you need to retire for yourself, and not your parents," I keep reminding him.

"Trying telling them that; when you reach your late eighties it is like dealing with children! I have to shout at father as he's so deaf."

"They should be in an old people's home," Anne piped in.

"My mother will not leave her cats behind! Anywhere she goes, her cats goes too!"

"You sure she wasn't a white witch in her former life?" I laughed. He was not amused.

The music started blasting away, causing Jonathon to roll his eyes in disbelief.

"She's a bit of a lunatic Jonathon. She talks to herself, and the cans of lagers you saw outside; it's all hers."

"What kind of creature has Bromford moved above you?" Jonathon asked. His words like lightening penetrated my heart. What kind of creature or thing did Bromford housing team moved me next too? A deranged white woman who claim they claimed love black men who

22

looked as if she had not washed for days or pressed her clothes. Was that how Bromford viewed black men? If Scot would not touch her with a barge pole what makes them think that she had a chance with the likes of me?

It was early in the morning, and the music started loudly again despite Cynthia's apology. I tried banging my pillow, tossing and turning, but the music continues blasting through the ceiling. Now I could hear her screaming profanities, followed by slamming all the doors as she walked through one door after the other.

I could not believe it. Bromford offered to me a tenancy agreement without warning me that there was a woman with mental health problems living above. Scot despite his dodgy dealings after all was right. I lay awake thinking how the landlady had the nerve to say that this vile animal loved black men! How could she have the nerve to insult me like that?

Bromford must have known what this woman was like as other tenants had moved out some lasting only two weeks and yet they had chosen to put a black man beneath this crazy woman! I perceived the move on Bromford part to be racist and insulting.

But I was not a quitter; but could I live beneath a woman that made so much noise without noticing it? Yet another night and I could not sleep. My living nightmares seemed to have begun. The music continued, and the slamming of doors right to the break of dawn.

"I can't live with this!" I moaned to myself now getting dressed.

While the water in the kettle was steaming, and the bright skies had stirred from her dark sleep, my attention was drawn to the post man dropping a letter through my door. I went to open it.

As I began reading the letter, I had to pinch myself. Bromford had written to me. Cynthia had complained about noise coming from my flat!

I was sure that this was a wind up; but it was all there in black and white with Bromford's official logo. The letter warned me of my tenancy agreement which I thought was a bit rich coming from them.

I left for work, when I saw Scot again.

"Morning!"

I grunted in return.

"Did she keep you up last night then?" Scot asked, with a knowing smile.

"She was at it since 3:00am in the morning," I replied still doped up by lack of sleep.

"Come on, I'll drop you off in town. That's where you're going isn't it?"

"Yeah."

Scot fastened his seatbelt, and so did I; and drove out of the car park.

"She will drive you out like she did the rest of them," he said sounding as if he was in bookies laying bets on to see how long I would last.

"Why does she get away with it?"

"We all signed up a petition against her, but Bromford Housing ignores them all. That woman has made people's lives hell since she has been there," Scot said his grin, showing his stained teeth and unwashed face. I could see that he was a smoker. His skin looked ailing yellow and his breath grey.

"So who were the previous tenants?"

"One was a single mother with a child, but she lasted one night. That was how bad it really got and she decided to just leave."

"One night?"

"Yes mate... just one night and that was too much for her she just packed and left."

"Does she get on with anyone in the neighbourhood?"

"You're kidding! No one likes her I! At least four people have had their cars dented by her..."

"...Why not call the police?"

"We can't prove it. But we know it's her who else is crazy around Perton? I'll give you £100 if you last one month."

"I'll last long enough to finish my music studies and move on. So how come you're still living two doors away from Cynthia and haven't moved out?"

"That's because I keep her sweet. I give her DVDs and music. So my car is safe. If I didn't give her those things I would not have a car!"

"So you are paying her protection by offering gifts?"

"Something like that Kevin there is no other way or my car might as well be gone tomorrow!"

"Well give her classical music and not dance," I said, as the car came to a halt.

"I knew it was too good to be true," I muttered.

"What is?"

"Oh... nothing. You would not understand Scot."

"Do you know another reason why she is untouchable?"

"You already said; the neighbours have no evidence against her."

"No... Much more than that, Cynthia's mother is a Magistrate judge so she has extra protection. There is also this police officer who is a good friend of the family who make sure that no charges are brought against her!"

"God Almighty," I said in disbelief," she has more protection than the Mafia!"

"See what I'm getting at Kevin? As long as she pays the rent Bromford will not do anything and she has internal contacts. The woman can't be touched! How can you argue with a Magistrate, and a police officer who is siding up with her? You don't stand a chance! All they do is just throw the complaint into the bin or drop the charges the next day. She can drive around drunk silly but no charges are ever brought forward! It is all mental!"

"It is illegal what they are doing..."

"...They are the law; they do what they want Kevin it is all hush hush..."

"...it is still wrong. They just have not been caught abusing the system! Anyway, See you around Scot," I manage to say; under the shock of what I had just heard.

I walked into the shop.

"Good Morning young man, you look like death warmed up!" Barry said.

"You would if you were kept up half the night."

"You want to complain against that neighbour of yours. She is being unsociable."

"Yes, I'll get on the phone to Bromford Housing."

"Anyway, we have some furniture's to budge from this big house. Oh my poor wrist is playing up today I must have sprained the damn thing."

"Do you want me to drive?"

"Do you drive?"

"Yes."

He tossed me the keys, "Get the old girl going. I'll be with you in seconds." I jumped into the big van and started it up. The engine rolled over but didn't sound too good to my ear, and was probably on her way out. It could have been the fan belt, or worse, the casket. I looked tall sitting so high above the pavement. It was different from driving a car that was so much lower. My boss showed up and jumped into the passenger seat; we drove off.

"I had to fetch myself sandwiches. My wife Dorothy made them last night. You've got a big appetite young man these ones are yours. She also made you some. She thought you'd being a student you wouldn't be eating well." I turned and smiled quite touched by their kindness.

Chapter Three

The noise showed no signs of stopping from above. I had tried ringing, and writing to Bromford Housing but to no avail. Cynthia was running riot around the neighbourhood, but I faced the worse; as she lived directly above my flat. My friend Darren was expected to visit me that day Sunday after Church.

I rose up from my bed; ran a bath and sunk into it the hot rippling bubbles. I closed my eyes as my muscular body slumped into the hot water, and now covered my ears. I could not hear the music now thumping out from above. I tend to do this a number of times a day! The noise was so bad that it was only by running a bath and putting my head under water that I could relieve myself from it for a few minutes! But this was fleeting as I rose up for air. After my bath; I was in the bedroom putting on my shirt and tie. I splashed some lotion onto my face, followed by my jacket and got ready for Church.

At the Pentecostal Church, I sat at the back; listening to the black preacher yelling about fornication, the sins of homosexuality, and the lust of the flesh; that he almost blew the PA system. The louder he screamed; the more praises and shouts of amen, choruses from the strong congregation. The preacher was only a small, but stocky built black man. He never did plan his sermon; there was hardly any order, he just went where the spirit led him and that could mean anywhere.

The sweat profuse off his forehead, he catches it with his white hankie; moving off the subject of fornication, now ranting on about the mark of the beast and the anti Christ. It didn't matter how illogical his preaching plan was, with feral rhythm, and the sporadic contribution from the drummer, ultimately the congregation would all lift off into strange tongues becoming like pandemonium extravaganza; or a free for all. I watched as the whole Church danced around the pew, rolling around the floor to the rhythm of loud gospel music, some looked as if they were competing at who could yell or skip the craziest.

One large black woman began flapping her arms as if she was a bird about to take off the ground, only to be restraint by another Christian holding her down. Did she really think she was going to fly off under the power of spirit?

It was all crazy; but that was my Church. This was your typical black Pentecostal Sunday where it was bursting with boogie down, nutty dancing where the doctrines need not make any sense just as long as you had your daily emotional release. It was this spiritual medication which kept black people sane in England during the racist fifties/sixties. But sometimes I wondered what I was doing there.

"The lord loves a cheerful giver," screamed the pastor, as if he had it timed well. Suddenly the lively atmosphere changes; the flock suddenly realised that it was money time. That was the part which they hated the most. No one liked to part with their money and be cheerful about it! But there was always sweet moving music playing from the musicians using their skill to get you to part with their money. God loved a cheerful giver the preacher kept screaming down the microphone.

But was it possible to part with a broad grin on your face while giving away money to the Church? It didn't make any sense to me.

"The Lord says prove me; see if I will fill your barns with new wine," he screams, noticing how the mood suddenly sobers up. "You can steal from man, but you can't rob God! I know there is a recession...!"

"...Praise the Lord!" The congregation agreed hoping he would back off now.

"...But in heaven there is no recession because God's bank has infinite money!"

"Yes!" The congregation yelled back in agreement.

"God has all the money for you waiting for you in his bank; all you need is faith to cash it today! How big is your faith today brothers and sisters? How much do you want to give God today?"

After what appeared to be fifteen minutes of hard-core unrestraint hustling from his congregation; the pastor led the Church into a closing prayer. He did not seem happy about the taking for that day as his eyes were not closed. There was a recession, and people were holding onto what they had even if the pastor claimed that God had tons of cash in the heavenly bank waiting for them to cash it by faith! No one in the Church yet had seen this infinite money became flesh.

Black Churches seemed to be nothing more than cultural gathering, lots of crazy dancing and a mishmash of religious text quoted out of context to cater for romantics who didn't question anything other what was told to them.

After Church service, the money I could have given my pastor I spent on a double cheese burger at MacDonald. Darrel walked in. Being Sunday, it was not that busy, only sporadic feet flickered past the window.

It was so different from the weekend when it would be a task just trying to grab a seat, and then forced to down my fries and milk shake because someone was eyeing up my seat. Darrel eventually joined me, holding his cheese burger and a hot pie. We touched fist, and he sat opposite me.

"So how the hell did you get that job? I'm still looking for one!" Before waiting for an answer from me, he began attacking his juicy cheese burger.

"Just being at the right place at the right time," I replied, finishing my drink through straw.

"If I had a pound for everyone that says that to me; I wouldn't need to work Kevin!"

"Well all I did was to go in to look for some furniture's, and this man was struggling to carry in some chairs so I helped him out. It turned out..."

"...That he was the owner! You are one lucky bastard!"

"Well they leave in two years; they're going to New Zealand or Australia to retire."

"Well by then Kevin," he said amid a wink, "you will have your music qualifications. Come on let's go to the pub for a pint."

I thought about it. It was Sunday; God's day; but either it was that or I go back home to the loud music. I decided that the pub was a better option. We finished off our drinks and left.

"Any pub in mind?" I asked scanning the street.

"We'll go to this one," Darrel replied pointing to a pub on one of the corners of the High street.

Darrel ordered the drinks, and then made his way over to me; carrying the two glasses.

"You want to ease off your studies a bit!"
"Why?"

"You look tired as if you haven't' slept in ages."
"Neither would you if you were living next door to a psychotic woman!"
"You should complain!"
"I have, Bromford Housing Association just ignore all my phone calls and letters. I even rang the emergency out of hour line and left messages... no one even returned my calls. I just can't work it out!"
"There are laws against antisocial behaviour!" Said Darrel, knocking back his lager.
"So your girlfriend has finally moved in then?"
"Yes."
"But I thought you wanted your own space. Wasn't that the reason why you moved where you did?"
I thought before answering his question.
 "Bromford has written to me," I said, ignoring my friend's question.
"Oh... and about time too! Hopefully it was about your psychotic neighbour from hell!"
"No... She made a complaint about noise coming from my flat," I replied.
"But you don't make any noise Kevin!"
"I still got a caution letter from Bromford Housing!"
"I think they've deliberately moved you next door to the Devil!"
"It looks like it."
"What are you going to do about it Kevin?"
"What can I do?"
"Move out brother!"
"Move out! Do you know how long it took me to move out the ghetto?"

"And look where they have moved you out too? Facing sleepless nights beneath a crazy alcoholic woman... maybe you are better off in the ghetto with your own kind bro!"
"Am I paranoid Darren?"
"What do you mean?"

"When I moved in; three white neighbours suddenly moved out in less than a week! I mean it was as if they were in a rush to move their things out using dustbins anything would do."

"Of course you're not!"

"What did they look like? I mean how old were they?"

"Young white girls with white boyfriends... mostly young people."

"They don't want a big gorilla living next door to their reserved virginal white girls. Who knows what she might do if her hubby is out at work, and she needs a plumber to screw her light bulb in," Darrell added with a knowing winked.

"Then how come my girlfriend didn't notice then? I actually saw them all in less than a few days moving out and yet my woman didn't even notice! Perton is so difficult to get into and yet they were doing a runner!"

"How do you know she didn't notice? Maybe she was too embarrassed to comment that her own people are that racist in this days and age!"

"I thought the white flight happened in the fifties Darrel not in the 21st century!" I said sounding rather naive. I was beginning to wonder whether having too many white friends was making me naive.

I was at home with my girlfriend watching television thinking over what my Friend had said in the pub earlier on. He had a point. I had been stung badly.

I should have known it was too good to be true. What black people ever had good white neighbours living next door to them unless they had serious money? The good ones or the poor whites who thought they were better than blacks ended up moving out. Black people were not even liked by white gay neighbours as I had experienced.

"Why don't you get some sleep Kevin, while she is quiet upstairs?" My girlfriend said looking up at the ceiling hoping that her words would not somehow magically wake her up. I looked at the television; there was nothing interesting on. I was just about to get up, when my neighbour started blasting her music out loudly. This caused me to roll my eyes with defeat saying, "Tomorrow I am going to see Joel the housing manager. This can't go on!"

"Well you know she said that she has been here seven years, and she's going no where. She wants to drive us out like she did the other neighbours," said Anne.

"Well we are not going no where... seven years or no seven years she is not driving me out of my own home!" I snapped loudly trying to compete with the loud thumping music.

*

The next Monday morning, I had arranged for one of Bromford staff to visit my home. I was sure that something would now be sorted out. I looked out of the window, waiting for the officer to show up. At last he arrived. I watched as the plump rounded bloke shuffle his way down the path looking unprofessional and not well dressed. Was he not being paid well? I knew there was a recession but surely Bromford paid their staff well enough to buy decent clothes at least? I could not understand how he managed to keep his professional job looking like he had just woken up and not bothering to wear respectable clothes for work.

He looked quite simple, shabby with a set smile on his mug. He looked down-and-out grubby, and something like a weasel. I was not expecting this blob arriving at my flat.

I spoke to Joel from inside my front door, telling him about loud music and the swearing and abuse that was hurled from above, but the words just seem to bounce back at me. Joel's face looked blank as a white canvass not drawing in anything. His dark eyes looked vacant like if he had just snorted coke.

"What do you want me to do about it?" He said, shrugging his shoulders, as if it was not his problem. I couldn't believe what I had just heard. Surely it was a joke or something that Joel was pulling; even though he didn't find it all amusing?

"The neighbours around here have told me that she is a nightmare! I want something done?" I pleaded.

"The courts won't evict her!" He said dispassionately. "The courts will not get rid of anyone from their flats. We have tried with other tenants."

I could not believe what I was hearing.

"Are you trying to tell me that I have to live next door to someone who plays loud music, and screams during the early hours of the morning Joel?"

"Yes."

"Thanks for nothing!" I slammed the door, and broke the news to my girlfriend. She was quite shocked by it all. As we talked about the problem, Cynthia started to bang her feet upstairs, and it didn't matter what room we went into, the noise would follow.

"She is not going to drive me out!" I said defiantly.

"She finds you a threat Kevin, because you have lasted here the longest!" Said Anne. "She drove the other neighbours out in less than one week; one being a single mother. But you're still here."

"There has to be something that we could do about it?" I said.

The music continued pumping away, ensued by stamping and swearing. It was as if some form of witchcraft or black ritual was going on above. The thuds and the beat just continued showing no signs of stopping obviously made by a maniac.

"I can see why you ask me to move in with you. The woman is dangerous. If she can't drive you out with noise God know what she could accuse you off!"

We both walked into the kitchen, and could see Cynthia sitting in the garden. She had cans of beer around her, just drinking away as if there was no tomorrow. Her face was sickly ashen and spotted, her clothes ragged and grubby. She just sat there talking to herself and laughing along as if someone was with her. The music was still pumping away from her flat.

"She's nuts!" whispered Anne.

"You're telling me!"

We watched from the kitchen window, as she tried to get up off the grass, but fell over. After numerous efforts, she managed to stumble onto her feet. She picks up her beer cans, spilling some in the process, and looking around; she stumbles back into her flat to the loud music. The music stopped playing. There was an inquisitive silence. Maybe she was changing the CDs? Or did she leave her flat to purchase further beers?

"Do you think she's sound asleep?" Asked Anne.

"I hope she's dead!" I snapped.

"Do you fancy a coffee?" She asked.

"Yeah I fancy a cup right honey."

I drank my coffee, when my mobile went off.

So the mornings and the evenings continued. Despite trying to get Bromford to Act; I faced high walls of strong silence. I could not understand why I was not getting anywhere despite written letters and the number of phone calls made to the Bromford office. I eventually gave in. I had no choice but to live with the noise above me.

I was now used to see Cynthia drunk on a daily basis; buying her booze and then staggering back to her flat not being able to resist the smell of liquor but consuming it hard before reaching her front door. Sometimes she would hurl abuse at me in front of my flat if the mood took her and then fell asleep on the grass clutching the bottle of alcohol.

Later that evening Cynthia recovered from her booze and knocked on our door.

"Shall I go?" Anne asked.

"No. I will." I said opening the door. Cynthia acted all shifty while struggling to regain composure.

"I have a surprise in store for you," she winks as she shuffles off. I stood there not knowing what she meant. Her words sounded menacing. Once sharing what was said with my girlfriend we dismissed it as nothing but idle talk.

But one evening approaching midnight Cynthia had really gone off the rails. It was around 1:00am when I and my girlfriend were both watching the God channel. The night was strangely silent almost unusual. No banging or screaming.

Something was not right. The mood in the air was expectant and yet I didn't know why. Maybe it was the ominous threats Cynthia had made leaving us both on edge?

I looked at my girlfriend lovingly for a second time as both their gaze seemed to just hold in a kind of dreamy state.

"Are you alright?" I asked yet again.

"Yes honey," She replied. I smiled. But something was not quite right that strange night. That evening an eerie supernatural presence searched the stillness of the flat the lights appeared to have additional illumination. It was a long time since I have seen this kind of urgency in the air.

That night; I didn't know why I ended up watching the God channel but I did. We sat back against the comfortable Italian leather settee.

Chapter four

"I can smell paraffin!" I shouted jumping up from the chair and racing towards the front door. "Call the police Anne, Cynthia has thrown a rag soaked with petrol through our letterbox!" I shouted looking at the burnt white net curtain which had been singe while the rag was on the floor. The flat was filled the smell of paraffin mixed with fear and atonal confusion. Cynthia had thrown petrol into our flat door with the intention of killing us both inside. Now I was in shock. My body became numb; I just stood there inhaling in the smell of fumes filling my flat not being able to feel my fingers.

"I knew something was not right!" I said turning to my girlfriend still visibly shaking.

The police arrived and took statements from the both of us. I had to guess what time I thought the petrol was put through my letterbox. While I was writing the statement my hands were shaking. Cynthia was going to set me on fire inside my own flat! I was finding it hard to cope with this. I glanced across at the God channel with the volume turned down on the television now.

"Why didn't the door go up in flames?" The officer asked looking more puzzled taking another look at the front door. It was lit; soaked in petrol; started to burn; but something or someone had extinguished it before it could spread any further and potentially leading to our deaths.

"You are very lucky to be here! I am still shocked that Bromford has not acted sooner," the police officer said.

"What do you mean?" I asked still in a dark horror movie; trying to make sense of it all.

"Well they have a duty of care in dealing with anti social tenants. This should not have come to this," the police officer said looking quite startled.

"She could have killed my cats!" I said, thinking about Lily, and her little kittens.

The police officer offered me a strange look when I mentioned about my cats.

"I will go next door and arrest her," the office said.

"You don't want to go alone!" I said watching him leave.

"Why?" He asked turning around waiting for an answer.

"She left me a message on my answering machine warning me that she had 'six "ucking knives" in her flat, and that she was not afraid to use them. She also said in her telephone message that it took seven police officers to restrain her to get her into the "paddy wagon," as she called it."

"Why is she not in prison if she is so dangerous?" The police officer asked.

"Because her mother is a magistrate and her policeman friend 'Desmond' always gets her off," Anne said jumping in now pleased to see that something was being done.

"Well I know where this Desmond is. He is on holiday so he will not be helping her with this one. We will wait until she calms down and bring some officers down. Thank for the warning Kevin."

"Not at all," I said.

That night I could not sleep. The endorphins in my body were doing somersaults making me so alert as if my own natural caffeine levels were intolerably high. I could not think straight.

Cynthia was upstairs; I knew that she would try it again if she could. She was prepared to do murder even if it meant to drive me out my own home! Despite the letters I had written to Bromford they failed to act and now it had come to me nearly losing my life.

"Look you need the sleep; I will keep watch; I will stay up for the night," said Anne. I was so pleased but I needed to sleep off the fear although I knew that the chances of me sleeping now were nil. How could I when someone tried setting me on fire inside my own flat? The first thing that I had to do was to ring Bromford and inform them what had happened. Bromford might not value my life; but their own property they were bound to be angry and do something at last if the police didn't beat them to it.

So many things ran through my mind while I was trying to sleep. I kept tossing and turning, followed by patting my pillow but still I could not sleep.

"Do you know," I said to my girlfriend, "we had to put our lives on the edge just stay in our own flat? We had to almost be burnt alive or just pack up and leave!"

"I know honey. But you must try and sleep; we'll discuss it in the morning," my girlfriend whispered stroking my hair as I was a child who needed nursing. She was a great comfort to me. Anne was so in control. I could not be sure what was going through her mind; was she not afraid?

"But why should it come to this! Why should I nearly lose my life to get Bromford to even act? Somehow it is not right. I feel as if I have no protection with animals having more protection than me. Anyone can do whatever they want to me as my black skin doesn't count for anything!"

"Don't work yourself up," pleads my girlfriend now showing more emotions.

"But it is true! Let me harass a white neighbour like Cynthia did to us and watch how quickly I get evicted!"

"I know. But what can you do?"

"What can I do? Nothing Anne... it is not my country... I might be born here; but it does not make me have any rights. I am not under the Queen's Peace. I am no one in England."

"You should not say such things Kevin you have as much rights as anyone."

"Yeah... maybe if I was white and gay... that is what England regards human rights to be today Anne...!"

Chapter five

The next morning my girlfriend and I listened to the loud noise in front of our flat. But this time it was not insults and verbal abuse... it was an army of police officers attempting to kick off Cynthia's front door.

"It's the Police... open up your door!" The officers shouted into her letterbox. Cynthia had blocked herself inside the flat refusing to open the door no matter how much they shouted for her to give them entry. She knew that she was in serious trouble now. She might be able to get away with anything where Bromford Housing association was concerned; and her Magistrate mother; but this was different. She tried to carry out an arson attempt in which to endanger a life. Cynthia was prepared to go all the way to have her way even if it meant taking a life!

Finally the police forced their way into her flat where she was arrested. She was led away in handcuffs not looking so invincible this time. There were no booze in her hands; she was not staggering; but looked sober. Was she intoxicated when she committed the attempted arson? She sobered up very quickly as she now had to face the music. I didn't see her fighting or resisting arrest as she claimed she had done in the past. I did not see her knives she claimed to have used on the police before despite never being charged! She went away quietly even if she did refuse to open the door to the police.

I could not believe that this monster was allowed to make not only my life hell but the neighbourhood. Her reign of terror had now come to an end.

She must have known what she had done as why would she barricade her door? She had the intentions to commit murder if driving me out with noise failed to do the job. Would I ever mentally recover from this frightful episode? The damage had been done.

I had survived living in the roughest parts of dark Wolverhampton inner-city area witnessing hard drugs being sold openly on the streets; even walking past gangs hanging around street corners; but never did I think that in such a leafy area as Perton that this could ever happen to me. I had faced not only a neighbour who tried to kill me; but a neighbourhood that felt that she could get away with it.

Cynthia tried to drive me out my flat resorting to arson. I also had to face a neighbourhood that didn't like seeing black people and a system that didn't want to protect me.

I had no protection from Bromford; neither for the harassment nor the noise pollution that I was made to endure. I was beginning to see that maybe being black in England had a serious price tag attached to it.

"Well now we will get some sleep for once," Anne said.

"Yes... peace at last," I agreed.

"I hope Bromford put some decent neighbours above," I said.

"After what we've been through they should," she replied.

"What do you think will happen to her?" Anne asked.

"Well she would not open the door to the police which is a sign of guilt. If they find evidence in her flat that she was the culprit then she will serve prison time. Bromford will not leave the flat open they will rent it out as they want their money," I said weighing up at the same time what I was saying.

"She needs help and she will find it in prison where she can't get her hands on any alcohol," Anne said.

"What gets me is why she was able to get away with it for so long," I said.

"You know it is because her mother is a Magistrate and her friend is a policeman. They always covered up her crimes," Anne replied.

"So what would have happened if her policeman friend Duncan was on duty?" I asked fearing what the outcome could have been.

"She would have got away with it... again," Anne sighs; showing raised anger in her voice. "So it is a good thing that Desmond was not on duty," she finished.

"Her mother's a Magistrate carefully covering up for her own daughter's crimes. She has no right to judge other people for their crimes. It just goes to show that you are protected when you know the right people," I said with reflection.

"It seems that way."

"Then maybe I should get a corrupt policeman as a friend Anne, and a friend as a magistrate and then I to will escape the law!"

Chapter Six

Bromford offices were opened after the weekend of sheer hell. I thought that the episode of the weekend would not only embarrass Bromford Housing Association but force them to evict Cynthia while she was awaiting trial. I was on the telephone waiting to talk to the housing officer. Finally I got through.

"Cynthia tried to commit arson attempt on my life. She has been arrested by the police," I said trembling. But what came next I was not expecting.

"You're exaggerating; Kevin she is not a bad girl," came the sarcastic reply.

"What! She was arrested for trying to burn me alive in my own flat!"

"I am sure it is nothing. She is a lovely girl really... quite harmless."

Those words uttered were too much for me to take now. I just slammed down the phone.

"They don't care!" I said turning to my girlfriend.

"They just want the rent," Anne replied not knowing what to say. But was it more than just rent?

"But the whole of their building could have gone up in flames! Let me try and set fire to one of their properties and see what happens! It must be because I am a black man and they don't care what happens to me! Well let us see what the Voice Newspaper has to say about the way they treat their black tenants!" I angrily said.

I eventually contacted a well known black newspaper: The Voice. I was sure that racism was the reasons as to why Bromford Housing Association didn't take any of my complaints seriously.

But I had to relive the arson attempt by telling my account to the female journalist. It was too painful for me as I found myself talking at speeds of 120 miles per hour not even catching a breath in between. I became anxious now and was showing signs of being moody. I was no longer laid back but preoccupied with racism and watching fires on You Tube. My habits were becoming unhealthier. Once telling my side of the story I was so relieved to get it off my heavy chest. I felt like a rat in a cage just running around in circles not being able to escape but maybe there was a sense of freedom about to emerge?

41

The newspaper had to get Bromford side of their story I was confident that they could not escape from this major blunder?

However, the next morning; I thought I was still in a deep sleep even though I had woken up. I held the newspaper for a while inspecting the photo they had from me. It took me some time to chew over what I was reading. Surely they would not have been so bold as to say that to the Voice Newspaper? Bromford Housing Association denied that any crime of an anti-social behaviour had taken place against me! I sank onto the bed not being able to breathe.
Despite Cynthia now in prison after pleading guilty and receiving thee and half years Bromford still stuck the knife into my back by calling me a liar.

They had told reporters that it was all in my mind. No such crime had taken place. I felt as if I was going to throw up. I was so angry and yet felt ill at the same time while confused.

"I heard what happened," said one of the neighbours in her sixties with a scrawny and wrinkled face. I was not sure whether she stopped me to offer her condolences or just to nose around.
"Bromford was still going to keep her here you know," she said.
"What! After what she done! But she is in prison!" I said not believing what I had just heard.
"Her mother refused to pay the rent that was the only reason why they let the flat go," she said.
The information was putting salt into my open wounds. What more could Bromford Housing Association do to me? I tried talking to solicitors; but neither of them would take on my case. They argued they had no social funding or used some technical reasons as to why they could not take it on. Bromford breached their tenancy agreement and yet there was nothing that I could do about it. I was not one of those rich men who were fortunate enough to sue someone for saying that they had foot bunion or acne.
Bromford had breached their duty of care and yet because I had no money the law didn't matter nor could it be enforced.

There appeared to be elements of racism involved and yet there was nothing that I could as it was Civil offence and therefore not in the public interest as according to one solicitor. I had nowhere to turn for advice.

"Well you did what many tenants failed to do," the old woman said; but I was not sure whether the tone of her voice was acrimonious.

"And what was that?" I asked.

"You got rid of her!"

"Got rid of her? That was not my intentions! She did that to herself."

"She was a very intelligent girl Cynthia; she was a member of Mensa you know. It is for people whose intelligence is way above the national average."

I listen to this old lady who seemed to be lamenting over the fact that Cynthia was now in prison. But it was as if her education compensate for her crime against a black man. All of a sudden the neighbourhood exchanged pleasantries over Cynthia as if she had graduated. I felt as if I had attended an awake for the deceased she became the hero I became the villain.

Her information regarding Cynthia's being a member of Mensa did shock me. But should that make her crime any less than if it was done by someone else? Was this grey haired woman trying to get me to feel sorry for Cynthia after what she had done to me? Suppose it was the other way around and I had tried setting fire to my white neighbour's flat; how then would she view my crime?

Everyone in the neighbourhood wanted me to see Cynthia as the victim. This became the game they now played. A black man gets abused, but the whites became the victim. No one spoke about the trauma that I had experience or how I could have lost my life. It was all about Cynthia's troubled past or her intelligence IQ. But if the white neighbours had a choice... would they rather keep Cynthia the arsonist and get rid of a nigger?

Why did this same community that had petitions to get rid of this dangerous woman suddenly wanted to keep her? What was all that about? Or were they hoping to use her as a lesser evil to force me out of my home and then deal with her later? For a few weeks I enjoyed peace and quiet in my own flat. Now that I had spoken to the Voice newspaper I was sure that Bromford would not treat me so badly in the future or would they? Would my contacting, The Voice Newspaper about my story becomes my worst nightmare? Would Bromford seek ultimate revenge against me?

Chapter Seven

I sat at the local conservative office with Sir 'Peter' he was quite stocky but for a conservative I was quite surprised that he did not seem to have the racism that I thought he would have towards me. Black people always voted labour as they regarded the conservatives to be racists and anti immigration but Sir Peter treated me like any other white candidate which immediately put me at ease.

I watched as he glanced at the Voice Newspaper.

"Oh that is you in the picture," he said as if I was some kind of celebrity but for the wrong reasons.

"Yes it is," I replied. My friend Jonathon said there silent probably mesmerised that he was in the company of someone with a title.

"Bromford are calling you a liar?" Sir Peter said. "Is this woman in prison for this alleged crime?"

"Yes she is Sir. She pleaded guilty without even a fight," I said.

"I will write to Bromford. I will go to the very top," he said. I left the building with my friend.

But this went on for a while as Sir Peter writing to Bromford and getting nothing back from them became routine. It appeared that Bromford was not going down without a fight no matter whom stood up against them title or not title.

Sir Peter would write to the top only to have his letters moved right back down to the same staff that was causing the problems. In the End Bromford seemed to have won that battle as temporarily they got Sir Peter out of the picture while they could inflict upon me their worse damage to come!

Chapter Eight

While Sir Peter was trying to get some sense out of Bromford; I however woke up early Sunday morning before 7am; to mannish drilling. My new neighbours had moved upstairs above me and were already moving around furniture. Everyone had a lie in on Sundays even the Prime Minister it was the traditional thing the world over but not above my flat!

7:00am and already there was banging and hammering and the moving of furniture despite the tenancy agreement stated that no noise she commence before 11:00am. The new neighbours had a clear four hours head start!

"That... is not looking good!" I warned.

"Give them a chance; they're only just trying to make themselves at home," Anne positively said.

"But 7:00am Sunday morning Anne? That does not make any sense to me as what considerate neighbours do that if they want to make a good impression?"

"Give them a chance," was all she could say.

I thought for a while about her comment. Maybe I was being too paranoid. I noted that there was a child cycling across the floor and there was ball bouncing making the sound like living hell. The noise became worse. Not once did they consider the neighbours who lived below them which I found odd! Something was not right about it all.

I looked out of the window and tried waving to the plump round faced blonde woman who moved upstairs with her equally chubby faced boyfriend, but she just gave me cold stares. She didn't seem to be surprised that she had a black neighbour which naturally most white people would secretly want to know.

But she was not taken aback; just cold stares. I did not believe in this multicultural Britain where white people moved in next to black neighbours and not even offer a flinch or some sort! Every black person was aware of the '**flinch**' experience whether travelling in an elevator or walking behind a white person on the street.

But this neighbour did not even flinch or gave away anything that she was shocked to have a black neighbour! Something was not right! Was I

46

being paranoid? You walk behind a white woman who is holding her handbag, and every black man experiences the 'flinch.'

You walk into a shop, and you get the flinch experience by staff or security guard who automatically on seeing a black face becoming defensive as black face means robbery it means thief it does not mean British citizen or human being... but this neighbour was not surprised! I was surprised they even wanted to move in! Something did not add up.

But this went on for **weeks**; the noise got worse and it now appeared to be deliberate!

"I am going to write them a courteous note asking them to consider us below," I said to my girlfriend.

"They should calm down. After all we did give them one of our wardrobes that we didn't need," Anne said.

"Yes... and they got rid of it in their green van almost immediately! That's gratitude for you!" I said.

I posted the letter. I was praying that another Cynthia would not be repeated. There was no way that I could survive another episode of noise and harassment. But something inside told me that this was only just the beginning; this was going to be something else!

But I began to witness 'Bailey' walking right across my grass almost as if he disrespected my defensive space and it was not just Bailey; but his friends and his family. They all walked across my piece of the grass right under my window in act of defiance as if I didn't exist. It was not a public right of way but it became just that. Throughout May we endured nothing but child cycling across the floor; ball being bounced up and down and now we could not have a sex life as it didn't matter how quiet we were the neighbours upstairs started banging. It became a joke.

What I could not understand was how his girlfriend who did not seem to be behind this; had nothing to say about his aggressive behaviour. Here was a white woman a minority group allegedly; witnessing his actions, and yet by her silence she condoned it. Would she have said something to him if I had been a white neighbour? When she first moved in; why did she totally ignore me when I said hello? Why did she not speak to me? What did her boyfriend had planned against me?

Chapter Nine

June arrived. But there were no signs of any improvements. I already had Bailey walking up to my window in a threatening way as if to offer me out. What was he trying to do? Suppose I reacted and took him on? What that his ultimate plan? My girlfriend was doing 14 hours shifts and having to come home to horrendous banging and ball being kicked about. This was putting a strain on our relationship now. I could not work out why Bailey's girlfriend said nothing about his behaviour. Here was a mother of a young daughter allowing this harassment to go on without even putting a stop to it.

And if Bailey's girlfriend would not do anything: there was no way we could turn as Bromford would just pass the ball and not take anything we said seriously. We even tried solicitors, but we had to have an enormous amount of money to pay for their services. There was nothing that we could do about this harassment, and antisocial behaviour; not when you were black and poor anyway.

The strain was showing now and I was afraid that it would lead eventually to physical confrontation, because they were flaunting their criminal behaviour not caring of the consequences which baffled me. What did they know that I didn't? How could they have the confidence to move above carrying out this deviant behaviour not fearing Bromford justice?

I was walking from the local shops when I stopped by my neighbour the nosey white haired lady.

"Did you hear the noise your new neighbours were making?" She asked.

"I know; it is hell having to live with it all over again," I replied being cautious of her. I remembered how she was defending Cynthia.

"It must be bad for you and yet I can hear it two doors away! You need to complain!"

"Why should I? They did nothing about Cynthia!" I said.

"You should complain. You won't complain because you are black! Don't let that put you off!"

I was embarrassed by what she had just said. I was caught off guard. I hated being caught off guard not knowing what to say next. She was not a political correct old white woman there was a reason why she said that but I could not put my finger on it.

"Have you heard anymore on Cynthia?" She asked breaking the silence.

"No. I know she is in prison, and that is it, with of course you telling me that Bromford would have kept her if her mother was willing to pay the rent," I said sounding weak now not the confident person I was when I first moved into Perton.

"Well it is true. Bromford was not going to evict her. They were going to leave the flat open for Cynthia to come back too but her mother was not going to pay rent while her daughter was in prison."

"So Cynthia's mother wanted the flat to belong to Cynthia... pay no rent on it; so when she is released from prison her daughter returns back to it?" I said.

"Something like that," the old woman said.

"And she calls herself justice?" I said.

"You saw her parents didn't you?"

"I did," came back my reply.

"They are very nice people. So middle class. I wonder where Cynthia went wrong!"

"Well... they never liked me. It was almost as if they would have preferred to have me burnt alive than to have their daughter in prison! It was like I was to blame for her being locked up!"

"The flat above you must be cursed," she said.

"Why?"

"It seems to attract nutters." We drifted into small chitchats for a while.

"I have been in Perton for 40 years, and can honestly say that it has gone downhill," she said. I said nothing. "Watch out for Scot!" She whispered looking across towards her right side.

"Why?" Not again. I thought to myself. Not another person who is Waco.

"He gets strange brown parcels arriving at his flat. Don't ask me what's in them; but I suspect it is drugs," she said tapping her fingers to her nose as if she was Miss Marple.

"Oh," I replied not interested.

"He needs to be reported to Bromford for using his flat illegal purposes," she warns me as if I was the one who was supposed to do her dirty work. Why is she telling me all this I wondered now? Am I the neighbourhood police man or something? Or was I just simply the neighbourhood black buffoon? If Scot was a drug dealer surely the neighbours would have had him busted by now?

"I have to go," I quickly said, sensing that she was trying to get me involved in something that I wanted nothing to do with.

"You keep away from Scot!"

"So what if he is selling copies of DVDs; everyone does it!" I now challenged letting her know I was not that naive to her tricks.

"That is what he wants you to think!" She replied defiantly.

I thought about what she had said. Scot was not the drug dealer type. He didn't make enough money and there was nothing in his flat that indicated otherwise. I wondered why she wanted me to keep away from Scot when the both of them were the best of friends! Maybe she didn't mind being friends with a so-called drug dealer?

"You keep well away from Scot!"

Her final words sounded as a teacher talking to a minor. But I shut my flat door behind me. Maybe he could warn me about her?

I didn't trust anyone in Perton as while on the one hand they claimed to be rivals with someone; the next they were seen linking arms in arms! Nothing was what it seemed; well to me any way. I was not going to get involved in people's dirty work only to find myself in the middle of it all. Maybe I was being set up for a reason; it just didn't add up.

"This noise is driving me mad!" I said to my girlfriend.

"I just did a twelve hour shift; I can't be putting up with you always complaining!" Anne shouted.

"You try being here all day listening to football being played above your head and bicycling moving across the ceiling!"

"What can I do Kevin? We can only report them to Bromford... again."

"But they won't listen," I argued.

"Have you been out at all today?" She asked me.

"Why should I be driven out of my own home? We pay out rent... my money is as good as anyone else's!"

"Because it will take the stress off our relationship when I return home," she said.

I walked into the kitchen to get some juice for Anne. She followed me.

The material inside the flat was so thin that it was easy to guess which room we were in. The sound proof was very poor so the neighbours knew how to follow us from room to room. It became unashamed aggravation but we as it seemed they knew they could get away with it.

"I can't believe that when we complaint Bromford said that the neighbours claimed they were not in when we complaint about their constant noise!" I said.

"They obviously don't care," Anne replied now sipping her juice. I watched as she drank it. I felt so emasculated not being able to protect her from the arson attempt and now not being able to do anything about the situation. I felt powerless not being able to do anything.

I had white neighbours above who were controlling my life; my moods and thoughts. They dominated what room I went into; when I could leave my flat; it became a game of chess for them as they were getting total pleasure out of watching me break slowly.

Chapter Ten

That week in **July 23** was bliss! There was not once drop of a pin or not even a cough. It was as if no one was upstairs not even the radio or television could be heard! There was no screeching sound of child riding her scooter upstairs above my ceiling... or football bouncing off the walls.

The noise machine; the council had placed into my flat did the job. I had peace of mind for seven days. I now knew the noise was intentional. They could be quiet if they really wanted too. If I thought the neighbours were going to kick off; I was set the recording.

Unfortunately the machine had to go back so I watched as the stout woman from the South Staffordshire council walked down the path to collect the machine my heart sank. What was going to happen now? Would my week of peace and bliss suddenly be faced with worse hell? I opened the door.

"How did you get on with the machine?" She asked.

"They were too quiet; I could not record even a single sound they were so quiet!"

"That's usual," she replied gathering up the cables.

"What do you mean?"

"They usually watch that is how they know," was her perceptive reply.

"Do you want some coffee?" I asked hoping she would stay longer so the peace and tranquillity would continue. Reading her mind I knew what she was thinking. She was a temporary noise bouncer for me. I could see the sympathy in her face.

"I'll have to go," she said as I watched her leaving and heading for the path. She was only half way down the path when the noise began! They were watching her!

I noticed that every time my door bell went the neighbours would happen to run to their door or open their windows to see who the visitors were. This became my life. How did they know that I had a noise machine in my flat? Who informed them in advance?

It was moving towards late July when my friend and I were watching world at war. The noise became so bad that I had to increase my television volume to the highest it would go! And yet Bromford said that I had angels for neighbours who didn't make a noise! And so Bromford would side track this no matter how serious it got.

"Didn't Bromford request you and your neighbour see a mediator?" My friend Jonathon said.

"But why... when they wanted us out from day one! Mediators are there for whites who have differences with whites not to deal with racism! Racism is a criminal offence not finding a solution having a cup of tea and sandwiches."

My white friend didn't know what to say to that.

"Bromford is trying to blame me as by introducing a halfway house then both neighbours gets the blame. What have I done Jonathon to have to sit with a bunch of racists? They don't want a black neighbour and will do everything to drive me out. Why should I have to sit down with haters as if I had any part in this? The Jews would not sit down to tea with the Nazi Germans discussing over Passover whether they maybe they were partly to blame for the holocaust... so why should I be blamed for living next door to white people?" I said.

"But what they are doing is against the law!" My friend screamed out loudly; trying to sound charismatic, but I wondered whether he was cracking up under the pressure.

"If you have the right money!" I bit back.

"Have you not contacted any solicitors?"

"They don't want to know. It is civil."

"Who said that?"

"Solicitors. The police say it is a landlord issue and not theirs so I keep facing some kind of institutional racism where I can't do anything," I said feeling depressed.

"What came of your Bromford complaint about the neighbours above," Jonathon asked.

"They were on the neighbour's side," I said.

What my friend said next shook me. I was not expecting it from someone like him. Not a patriotic man who taught English history lesson and where the word racist did not go anywhere near his lips.

"Bromford's attitude to you is clearly racist! They would not treat me like that as I am white!"

"What!" I asked pretending not to hear.

"They won't help you as you are a black man. They only gave you this flat as their intentions were to put problem white people above you as that is they think black people deserve. They would not do that to me," he said; with pride his head held high to relish the moment of white acknowledgement.

His words shook me up. Would I ever have decent white neighbours? It seemed that most decent white people had already taken their white flight while the worse types were left behind to live in black neighbours because maybe they had little choice.

The idea of labour's happy multicultural Britain was a fraud I began to see. Everyone was only happy as long as they could not see black faces.

The more extreme racists didn't want to see black people in England full stop.

I thought back to all the white neighbours I have had in the past; some were prostitutes, while the others knocking on my door asking if I sold pot! I must sell something illegal as in their eyes all black people commit crime. So they would not be too fussy who they had for neighbours as black people knew where they could get high and where to buy cheap cannabis.

It was almost as if the system had designed it to be that way. All the whites with problems were left in the ethnic neighbourhoods surrounded with crime and little opportunities and with no education. The number of times that I got stopped by professional white people asking if I knew how to break into their cars as they had locked themselves out, or University students soon to be lawyers or politicians; crawling like swamped ants into black neighbourhood craving cannabis or crack assuming that the first black man they set eyes upon was a dealer since he was an infant, was horrendous! They would stop you in front of your mother or your granny and think nothing of it.

And then you had the dodgy white van driven by white males packed with stolen televisions and dodgy dvds; only stopping black men assuming that we were all criminals was also embarrassing.

You could not leave ASDA or Netto without some strong accent gypsy stopping you thinking that because you were black you were into knocked off imitation Rolex watches. That was the only time when white people wanted anything to do with black people always on a criminal level. This was the truth of multicultural England based on nothing more than stereotyping and illegal wheeling and dealing.

Saturday 26 July I still could hear constantly the child above banging on the floor as if she was hitting the hammer on it. Her parents did nothing to stop her at all. I was sure that the child was put up to doing it.

Once the banging had stopped the scooter then took over racing along the floor above me. It got so bad I had to put my headphones on and listen to loud music now all I could hear were little thuds and child screaming even with my headphones on! No human being could have lived with such high levels of noise and yet Bromford did nothing. I had enough I decided to go around to Scot flat to see what could be done.

His flat had nice television and computer.

"One of my relatives died and left me some money so I am decorating," he said trying to excuse the paint and overalls. Apparently I was told by the old lady that he was always decorating. So where was he getting his money from? At that time I was not really bothered.

"You're here because of the noise," Scot said.

"I can't cope anymore. Will you join forces with me and complain to Bromford?"

My question forced him to choke on his cold drink.

"I can't. I can't get involved!" He said almost sounding like a whimpering dog.

"Why... why can't you do anything with me?"

"I went to school with Bailey. So I can't!"

I was not convinced. He kept Cynthia sweet claiming to be giving her cds but how was keeping Bailey happy? What was he giving to him? Bailey was always high he didn't seem to have to go very far to get his fix!

*

It was now evening and my girlfriend was home. I said nothing to her. We no longer communicated the way we used too. The relationship was now affected for the worse. I wanted to share my experience with her but she didn't want to come home to my whinging. We got ready for bed that night not saying much. I was breaking slowly; but I was sure that my girlfriend was in denial or she could not handle the situation.

If I was a tree every day; I was being chopped down from the root with an axe of their racism. As each blow undermines my inner strength I began to weaken every day slowly but surely it was only a matter of time when I would break.

Racism in England was an invisible strong wind which I felt in my life, forcing things out my way uprooting my houses from their foundations... causing chaos I can see, but the soul the evil I could not see his face. As he had many shapes, and too often changed his disguises. I never knew how or when I was going to be attacked next.

I was once a proud English man; joining national trust, having a fascination with British history and how they lived. I even called myself an English poet as that was the language I used in my sleep. Now I was just a nigger trying to make sense of where did I fit in this country where most whites did not want blacks for neighbours? Should I continue to try and integrate with those who hate my being here? Should I learn the English language to see the Queen as my own?

Chapter Eleven

29 July that morning started off quietly. In the silence my girlfriend got dressed; brushing her teeth and putting on her carer's uniform. The same routine every morning; nothing much different. We didn't say much just seem to be waiting for the noise to begin. We didn't need to set our alarm clock in the morning as without fail our neighbours above would make sure we were up and at night they would only allow us to sleep when they ran out of steam making all that noise! We were in a prison them being the officers who took control over our lives. We could only move from room to room should they wish or the noise level would be so loud forcing us to know who is in control.

That morning I did something unusual. I was watching my girlfriend walking down the path. I just started to become concerned for her safety. I was sure that if Cynthia could resort to arson then what would these neighbours resort next? There was melancholy presence like a dark cloud hovered over my girlfriend. I watched as she like a once blossoming flower suddenly lost her beautiful bloom. She no longer sparkled but began aging too quickly; her grey hairs sprout over night. Now we didn't smile so much like we used too. She worked hard but had to come home to my whinging and moaning and banging along with child screaming.

Anne looked back up at the neighbour's window. I wondered why she would do this. But as soon as my girlfriend left the car park the noise became horrendous! They were waiting for her to leave!

I could do nothing as I was already depressed from the arson attempt and now had to cope with this. I was losing hope in life and was beginning to lose strength to cope every day. They kept chopping at my tree waiting for it to fall... Now I knew it was harassment it was clear as night from day but what could I do about it? The police didn't want to know; Bromford claimed they were model neighbours and the noise council carried machines inside the flat that could be seen a mile away. No one could come to my home without the neighbours above watching. I became a prisoner in my own home and my mental health was rapidly deteriorating.

I hated the slightest noise as I had lived with it since Cynthia and now the new neighbours. I was afraid now that I would do something stupid. Suppose I was being driven to kill the bastards? I imagined my hands around his throat squeezing the life out off him until I could see the whites of his eyes closing and the soul leaving his racist body. I never hated anyone so much during my entire life. My relationship with white people changed drastically. I suspected most of them now and didn't trust any of them.

I always waited for some racist joke to come out or receive bad customer service. It made me become secluded and afraid. I was not the person that I was before moving into Perton. I became sensitive seeing racist behaviour in white people wondering if they knew that I already beat them to it. I knew what they were thinking. I am a dumb nigger, a thief, a robber, a drug dealer; I had many children from different women. I thought this before their eyes could tell me what they thought of me. I was cracking up. I was dying inside daily.

"Could I speak to Anne please," asked my girlfriend's boss. I waited. They were so used to me ringing Anne sometimes three times a day at her work place.
"What do you want?" Anne asked.
"I am suicidal. I can't cope anymore; they're driving me nuts Anne. I feel like either killing Bailey or myself!"
"You're talented Kevin! That is what they want you to do and then they will win! Don't play into their hands! You can't ring me ten times a day you will get me the sack!"
She said. I knew my girlfriend was right but they had already won. They were white and they knew it. I called my girlfriend at work sometimes ten times in one day! If I didn't I would have hung myself! I was suicidal. I could not cope with the noise the banging the cycling above the wind of invisible harassment which created chaos and destruction but the ugly face of racism carefully concealed.
"What can I do?" I asked with a broken voice.
"I will be home," she said. "I will have to go or I will get into trouble. You can't keep ringing my work place!" She put down the phone.
I thought of Bailey and his brawny skin head walking across my grass looking like they were on a Nazi rally of some sort. They were your

typical racist looking football hooligan but I had so much anger at times I wished they would attack me just so that I could unleash my fury; I was sure I would kill one of them even if it meant I died myself or ended being locked up for defending myself against a group of white male racist which has happened to black men in the past.

But I was not going to become another victim like Stephen Lawrence; I was too big; too strong physically.

But the games the neighbours were playing were all mental; because they were cowards. They were like a pack of hound dogs who hunted in groups and not alone being your typical bullies. I had never seen a racist operating alone; he or she was too cowardly.

15 August my girlfriend had swollen glands she had very high fever. I was so worried that while the noise continued I used a broom stick and began continually banging the ceiling. I was not going to have her put up with that when she had a temperature.

"What is your problem down there?" Bailey shouted down.

"If you want to fight me why not be a man about it! Stop being a coward" I shouted back loudly.

But my banging and offering him out at that moment worked. They were quiet for the rest of the day. Just the peace my girlfriend needed. I knew it would not be long before they started to up their antics again. But at least for get some well needed sleep.

August 16

The neighbours were more devious than I first anticipated. I noticed that during the last few mornings the neighbours would bang so loudly; until they realised we had woke up because as soon as we let the cats out the noise stopped.

As I suspected they dictated when we awake and when we go to bed! I was shocked that someone could hate another neighbour so wickedly that they would try everything in their power to ruin their lives. I could not understand the psychology of racial hate or what would drive a person to do the evil that they do. There was something irrational about evil that was so perverse and sinister where flesh and blood could watch with utter pleasure the decline in mental health of a fellow human being.

I took the atrocious crossing back in time where human cruelty cut deeper than a double-edged sword where so-called saints turned a blind to the Jewish holocaust or the African slave trade while not lifting a finger to do anything about it.

By any means necessary man was capable of digging deep from within his being and unleashing the most brutal of pain to another human simply because something inside him told him that blacks were not human or the Jews were Christ killers and loved money.

There was something in most white people that did not want black neighbours to even open the front door and see black faces. So many of them were not shy of packing their bags and moving off to New Zealand which many white patriotic called the country that is all whites, where Peter Jackson filmed Tolkien's 'Lord of the Rings' about a spiritual battle between light and darkness.

New Zealand was the mother of all mirrors of old Empire England. But when the English went into India and Africa not as neighbours but to challenge existing cultures and enslave the natives, people who lived there had to put up with it, and the legacy of what the British did in those areas is still seen today.

But ignorance is bliss. As the English could go anywhere in the world and settle there: whether it be: Barbados, Jamaica, India, Montego bay, West Indies, as they built houses there... transfer their pensions converting into sterling, and live like white kings and queens while the natives serve them until they expired.

But here in England, with wild season weather, and rare sun; I had neighbours trying to drive me out of my own home, while they had no problems settling in the homeland of my ancestors! They had no problems seeking sun tan in the homeland of my parents! It did not made any sense to me.

I would read on Perton Walls on the streets 'Paki or Niggers go home' probably written by children or adults with little education not seeing the hypocrisy in their attitude.

England was my home; although the cold streets I walked on told me I was a stranger from out of town. But when my eyes first opened; it was England that I saw. The first songs that I enjoyed were Christian hymns, and even loved Elgar's stirring tune 'land of hope and glory' which I played on the piano. My first kiss was with an English girl; my experience; my life; I would have thought would have made me an English man. How wrong I was!

I could not be British or English living next door to decent white people. I became like a freed slave to uppity where I had forgotten my place.

Chapter Twelve

August 22 My girlfriend and I were at the Wolverhampton harvester. One of our favourite restaurants in the area, because of the arrays of colourful mouth watering green salad with sweet barbeque spareribs and Jack Daniels sauce always cheered me up. It was only five miles from Perton so after cycling sometimes we would go there. But that day we drove.

The weather was so hot that quite a few people were either having a glass of wine or eating outside.

We scanned the menu and once deciding what we would choose the waitress sauntered over and took our orders.

"You can help yourself to the salads," she said taking the menu card cards from us.

Once arriving back at our tables we tucked into our salad of fresh cucumbers, corn, honey mustard slapped richly with lettuce and cold unlimited pasta.

"I still think that it was our new neighbour that stole our bicycles," I said.

"I know; but we can't prove it though."

"It is interesting how when they first realised that we informed the police; Bailey ran downstairs straight to the van and got rid of his vehicle for weeks! I think the bicycles were hidden in his green van," I said drinking a mouthful of pineapple and lemonade mixture which the waitress had just brought over.

"I know," Anne said not saying much.

"Those bicycles never went missing until they showed up and suddenly they disappeared! It does not add up. They must have stolen them... pack of thieves!" I said angrily.

"Plantation platter?" The waitress called out carrying over the two steaming hot plates.

"That is mine," thank you I replied glowing with an open smile. The food looked delicious as always. Anne had the steak medium rare. We tucked into our meal.

Only the harvester had that positive effect on me. Their meals were always delicious; the chicken tender and moist and their own unique sauces were out of this world. Of course you had the unlimited mouth watering salad to choose from...

"I tell you something Anne. Have you notice that every time you and I get into a serious argument the noise upstairs stops. It is almost as if they are getting aroused by it," I said.

"Maybe they want to split us up as you are with a white girl," she replied.

I thought on her comment. She was far from the truth.

"You're wrong Anne; their problem is they don't want a black man living underneath them. Why did they take the flat above us? I don't know it is just beyond me; it is as if the whole thing had been planned."

"Look let us just enjoy our time away from the flat," she said.

"I rather not go back!" I said.

This became our lives where we hated going back to the flat but spending time away from it. We would drive for miles not caring if we arrived in Scotland just as long as we were not home.

After our meal we drove back home. Anne and I were walking towards our door when Bailey's dog ran up towards her. I stood there frozen as I watched him pushed her with his elbow aside and picked up his dog.

That was too much for me there was no way that I could have done that to his girlfriend, and not have the police beating their chest and banging at my door. And yet he had the power to do it to assault my Mrs. We walked back into the flat. I knew there was going to be tension now.

"You see what it is like being a black man in England!" I shouted loudly that I was sure he could hear every word. "He can assault you before my very eyes confident that if I hit him I am the one who will get in trouble! He can assault you push you as he likes as I am nothing in the eyes of the white English law. I am still a slave!"

"I know this country is racist," Anne said. But I was too angry to listen to her one single comment.

"What man can push another man's woman in front of him and not feel emasculated? If you want a fight Bailey let us come outside and find a secluded area just me and you no witnesses!" I screamed out loudly that I thought I would faint. I was dizzy with anger ready to explode. The room was like black dots just rotating around faster and faster. The pressure and the intensity increasing as he started to verbally abuse my girlfriend out of the window whenever she went to the car. But these were model neighbours from heaven that Bromford said were angel of light! But where did Bromford get them from? Why would they put something like that upstairs above me knowing what I had been through with Cynthia? Was it deliberate?

Bailey now walked in front of my front window offering me out in broad daylight in view of the white neighbourhood. But it didn't bother him that his aggression could be seen as a public affray. Why was he not afraid?

"You're white Bailey the law will go on your side," I said opening the window.

"Let's go the graveyard; no security camera just me and you and the dead as witnesses. Name your time and place and I will be there dead or alive!"

"Bah!" he growled as he walked back into his flat.

Since my girlfriend had been assaulted by Bailey they had become extraordinarily hushed!

The screaming and football just ceased! Not even a pin could now be heard as I had time now to listen to the breeze as I opened my window something I had not done for a while! When the sun was blazing hot; I no longer had to leave the window closed having to endure sweat summer socks and flies not having an exit.

Bailey knew that he had assaulted my girlfriend and now the tension was on him for a change.

Chapter Thirteen

My girlfriend and I decided to press charges against Bailey. We however thought about the consequences. We knew that he had some hefty skin-heads who came to visit him but that was not going to no longer put us off.

However, once the police approached our neighbours; Anne decided not to press charges as she said that they would only deny the assault. She pulled out at last minute! Now as a result the noise began worse than before and their antisocial behaviour became evident.

Now the neighbours were smoking pot being drunk and abusive and neglecting their daughter who was screaming day and night and never seem to have a normal childhood that most children had. She did not seem to eat well or had regular sleep patterns just mayhem in her little life. It was no life for a child. The stench of thick green cannabis snaked its way out the window as thick fog to the music playing godlessly at all unrestraint hours.

This chaos began until early hours of the morning! Now I was afraid for my girlfriend's safety. I did not know how evil they could be whether they could match Cynthia. Now I used to just watch out the window every time my girlfriend went to work and when she returned.

I just could not understand why my girlfriend had to drop the charges as I was having peace and quiet. The police telling the neighbours that the charges were dropped did not put them on their best behaviour instead they wanted blood... mine!

21 October 2008. It was a cool autumn coloured evening with traces of roaming clouds with rows of tree leaves dying off. I drove to the round about when suddenly a green van shot right out from the left despite it being my right of way. We almost collided. I realised that it was Bailey. I steered the car into the car park when I noticed Bailey thick sour face growling and edging towards me. This was going to be the show down I thought to myself.

This was what it was all building too now it was going to be wars of fists rather than words. I looked at his rusty round white face; but it was the whitest I have ever seen. It didn't matter how many visible blemishes he had on his skin or the corroded texture of his facial line; he was still white. Despite Bailey wearing ragged jeans, and crinkled baggy shirt he was confident. He was on white territory with twitching curtains being moved by white neighbours reminding him.

I wore a smart jacket and matching trousers; but I was a black man in an all white neighbourhood. I wanted to so much for him to advance towards me but then I realised that maybe it was not a wise move. If Bailey struck out at me first who would the police arrest? What would any potential witnesses have to say about the incident? Could I take this kind of chance in a country that likes to boast that all men are equal and yet showed very little evidence in supporting the rhetoric?

"Who the 'uck you think you are" he growled.

"It was my right of way," I challenged.

"I aint scared of yow!" He said hoping to get me into a fight.

"Throw a punch then Bailey," I said; "See how long it takes me to blow your lights out!"

I shouted causing further twitching of neighbour's curtains like something out of a Clint Eastwood movie. It was just me and Bailey all the cowards were in doors.

"Are you threatening me? You think I'm scared of you!" He called me every name under the sun hoping to get me to hit him. But somehow I sensed it was a trap. Maybe if I had lashed out he would have called the police and got me where he wanted evicted and possibly in custody?

His girlfriend came out the van and took him away by his arm as I stood my grounds. It was foolish of me but I had reached my limit.

I was not bothered anymore about the CPS which happened to discriminatorily prosecute false claims against black men.

I got the police later involved that evening as I was confident that the incident was racial harassment from the outset. However, I was shocked that Bailey argued that I had threatened him in front of his three year old daughter! The police cunningly advise me not to pursue the charge against Bailey and he won't me!

I felt bribed and black mailed by the police. I was on the telephone talking to Jonathon. I explained the car incident which led up to the argument and then the police with the outcome.

"Are you sure you didn't see Bailey's daughter?" My friend quizzed.
"Jonathon only he and his girlfriend walked away! I would never argue in front of a child! Not even his!"
"It looked like they lied! What a cunning lot they are!" He said.

"After we argued Jonathon; I went back to the window and I watched him bringing in a mattress and still no child and yet I could hear her upstairs. I watched them both the whole time!"
"They must have left her alone upstairs in that flat which is against the law!" Jonathon said trying to sound like a lawyer or charismatic it didn't suit him he was too weak when it came to dealing with his own problems.
"They are always leaving her alone by herself," I said feeling sad that the police had done nothing.
"The police didn't want to do anything Kevin. So they just hushed it under the carpet hoping it would go away."
"I wonder if the police told him to countersue." I asked with a suspicion to my voice.
"Well it means less paperwork for them," Jonathon said.
"Or they are not interested in racial motivated crimes. It is just strange that the police told me that if I pursue a charge against Bailey he would also me. It sounds like the police are blackmailing me!"

Towards late October My girlfriend was doing her NVQ against the background of shouting and abuse. The whole scenario of her going off to work and the noise suddenly escalating became evident.
I hated having to admit that racism was the main factor as white people accused black people of using the race card but the evidence was staring me in the face. Why did they try to drive me out off my home? Would they have created this noise from hell having I been white? Society had now embraced homosexual cause; they became the new victims and quickly rallied sympathetic supporters.

Our television screens were filled with androgynous or homosexual males who turned social stony attitudes towards their favour. The government were even going wild and crazy over legalising gay marriages showing social attitude has changed so much. Everyone wanted a gay friend it was a trend these days. No one was even ashamed to bring home someone who was that way inclined or live next door to one but being black was different.

Still I felt guilty for daring speaking about my pain. When it came to racism it was now trendy to bury it or a find another language to subtly undermine the experience. Black people had given up fighting against racism so they seldom reported bad customer services or when they went for job interviews and seeing the shock on white people's faces on seeing them entering the building. It was pointless using the law when you were a victim of racism unless of course you happen to be white.

As for tribunals that were set up and run by whites they spent their time making sure that black people who were either murdered in police custody or unlawfully dismissed from employment; did not get any compensation. The English law and governing bodies I began to realise was nothing more than a piece of paper.

I was being harassed and race seemed to be the cause and yet I had no protection not from the police or Bromford. There was nothing that I could do.

Chapter fourteen

December I returned home that day from the steam room, when my girlfriend Anne looked as if she had seen a ghost. She was pale white, gaunt looking and shaking.

"What happened?" I thought fearing that she had been assaulted by Bailey yet again.

"They were banging and noisy for seven hours!" I listened to her... smiling wickedly inside. Now she knew what I had to experience for the last seven months.

"Every room I went into they followed me into it!" She said.

"They thought you were at work Anne," I suddenly said as if hit by a bolt of lightning.

"They are harassing you because you are black," she said almost fearing saying that B word.

"There is nothing Bromford Housing will do as I talked to the newspapers. As far as they are concerned my name is shit."

"We are going to have to give them what they want and move out," Anne said.

Anne now wanted action because she had experience only seven hours of hell; when I had to live with it.

"What... with five cars and two guinea pigs? No landlord private or Housing will touch us!"

"But we can't go on like this... you can't go on like this. You are not the same person I met! You have changed!"

"Of course I am not! I have had a neighbour tried to end my life with arson, and now racist neighbours don't you think it would change me a little? Ever since I reported Bromford to the Voice newspaper they have had it in for me!"

I was reaching depression stages and feeling suicidal. I had no purpose in life anymore. I didn't trust white people. They gave us the crap neighbourhoods or some crack smoking white neighbour living next door to them. Everything whites did had a sinister motive where black people were concerned. I was very angry. I had white friends and yet I didn't trust white people in general.

My mental health was in fast decline as I never felt so black and exposed and vulnerable at the same time. It was as if my skin was breathing not my soul... but my colour had taken on a life of its own. As around lower middle-classed Perton my skin was first to be seen and to quickly be judged.

No one really wanted to get to know me but judge what they saw on televisions or read in magazines. I began to wish that my skin colour would disappear where I would wake up in the morning only to find that I was not black... but white. And all of this was just a white man dreaming this black nightmare; but it was all too real the pain was there.

I was not white this was the black man's hell on earth. My black skin could not pack its luggage to go on a sunny holiday, or to have time out to chill and experience happiness for a while without having to carry around this evident burden.

The sound of my footsteps strolling around the local supermarket appearing louder and attracting hostile white gazes, becoming intense as head turning reveals hate that was all too common. But I had to live it out there were no escape. This experience no white gay or lesbian could ever relate too so I began to feel angry and bitter that my pain would be dared to be compared to their wants of social lavishness.

Everyone wanted to hang around gays and lesbians even party at their clubs... watch them on television as there were no social stigma. I became resentful of that fact. No one grumbled when there were effeminate men bombarding our screen or the number of gay or lesbian presenters. They were white and in England that was all that mattered.

11 December

Having rang the law society I was given a number of contact details of solicitors who they claimed could help me. But I ran around the block making phone calls after phone calls chasing numerous so-called experts on the law, but yet not one could help me at all. I was worn down.

One solicitor claimed that what was happening to me was a criminal offence and therefore a police matter while others were saying it was civil, and therefore a civil matter, but yet would cost me money as there was no funding when it came to civil litigation.

I could not understand how if racism was a criminal offense why I had to take out a civil? But from day one I was being given a dry carrot dangling in front of me as a stripper teasing her audience offering nothing more but an aroma of her silky-smooth knickers. The system became nothing more than this silky knickers set up to entice punters to spend money for nothing more than just sniffing three minutes paperwork and nothing more.

I must have called around all the firms in Manchester and Birmingham yet not solicitor was interested. It was fobbed off as a tenant and landlord issue and if they were experts in that area then they were in the business of defending landlords.

I stood no chance. Because system had invisible walls and glass ceiling that was built in such a way that the laws appeared fair but trying to seek justice for racial crimes became impossible and intentionally so.

I was on the phone to a solicitor in Birmingham explaining what was happening to me and how I could not find any solicitors to help me. But I was so incoherent and speaking quite quickly I was sure she didn't understood me. I had to repeat this over and over again to different solicitors that it was wearing me out...

"It's institutional racism," she confidently said.

"What do you mean?" I asked pretending to be quite shocked but I already suspected that.

"Institutional is defined when an organisation closes their ranks, and you seem to be banging your head against brick walls."

"What about my situation with my neighbours?" I asked.

"It is clearly racial harassment and it is a criminal offence. You need to go the police but they will try and fob you off but don't let them do it! Turn up at the police station if you have too!"

"Would you take on the case?" I asked pleading inside that she would. I needed so much a breakthrough. I was desperate now.

"I am an immigration solicitor."

"Okay," I was so sad that she could not help me my spirit slumped again.

"Let me warn you. One of the tactics of racist neighbours is to make counter claims against you so that you will drop your complaint against

71

them. Don't fall for it! Your landlord will even tactfully advise them to do this!"

"It already happened," I said, "And I was forced to retract my complaint!"

"More than likely the police planted suggestions to them to make counter complaint against you," she said sounding as if she had come across this deception before.

I was so saddened to hear this. Now there was no where I could turn my hopes were dashed against rocks washed out to sea. I thanked her for her helpful advice. I knew it was racism but to hear it from an expert made things different.

It was not a war without a purpose; it was because I was black. They didn't want a nigger living below their flat especially when the piece of garden at the front belonged to me. I took her advice and contacted the police. I was asked the usual nonsense of whether I was in any immediate danger and given a crime number. Whether they were going to do something was another thing. But I was not going to hold my breath.

I remembered my late Gran sharing a story with me about a black youth who was going through racism by white neighbours and how they tried to set him up for crimes that happened in the area. Her last days were spent in an old people's home where she was a victim of racial abuse by white elderly people. She refused to eat going on a hunger strike where later she died.

Even with old age where white people's flesh grew feeble and fragile; their racism still flames alive and will never simmering for one moment. Their skin might age; but their hate still burns the stronger and they carry it even to their graves not caring whether they will be judged for the evil that they do!

Chapter fifteen

It was Christmas day the carols singers were out in full force; the vibrant festive lights dazzling and the houses decorated around Perton. Even the local shops in Perton all boasted tints and tinsels with balloons and Father Christmas pictures putting people in the good mood to spend what they could not afford.

There were children knocking on doors singing Christmas carols. My own door as if they knew they avoided. I was not deserving of their rendition of the carols. As I could hear the carols silent night being sung it left me badly broken the children's haunting tune left me in further depression. My girlfriend tried to make me happy that morning but this was one Christmas that was not going to be a season of good will to all men. Would Bailey on that day bring peace on this saviour's day? Would he do it for his daughter at least?

I notice there were no decorations in his flat; his front door steps still winter cold no emotion no spirit of Christmas. Maybe it would be different inside?

My girlfriend had to work that day so I was alone watching television. I heard a car pulled up in the car park so I looked out of the window it was Anne. As she walked down the path I noticed she looked up in shock red faced.

"Merry Christmas," I said. We kissed.

"Have you notice Bailey and his skin-head mates hanging around," she asked.

"Ignore them Anne it is Christmas," I said shocked at myself.

"As I was walking down the path one of them shouted look at that fat cow!" She said

I was hurting I didn't mind them hurting me, but not my Anne. This was something else and not on Christmas day. All I could do was to delete the incident from my head and pretend I never heard a thing. What else could I do? Even the magic and spirit of Christmas could tame the wild beast of racism.

January

10 days into the new year and there were no signs of calm after the wild storm. The neighbours became more devious. They wanted us out badly; we had lasted too long and this year they were going to make sure that it happened no matter what. Our lives were made a living hell. First we had Cynthia trying to drive us and when that failed resorted to arson and now the new neighbours!

The slightest laughter my girlfriend and I made would be faced with the ceiling almost caving in on itself! We could not even share a laugh anymore! As for love-making that was thrown out of the window ages ago we were not allowed to make love or to laugh we were being controlled like robots! It became a deadly game of mind control.

But each time that Bailey stirred arguments between Anne and me they would be quiet for the whole day not even a mouse would be heard! I could never work out the motives? Many times I had a serious breakdown and wanted to go and kick off his door but Anne would hold me back crying her eyes out reminding me that I was a black man walking into their deadly trap.

I discovered that as the immigration solicitor predicted the neighbour were also complaining of noise which we never made! Now I had a severe mental breakdown. My body could no longer cope with the slightest pin drop. I was shaking out of control and on the edges of nervousness like someone smoking crack all day long. I didn't recognise myself. My friends were sick and tired of me talking about my pain that I was going through so I felt alone. The stress got to me so badly that I lost my voice and had to go into hospital! I had no choice but to seek mental help. I had to go to white people to diagnose medication to help me deal with racial harassment.

As for the government funded race relations organisations phones were answered by either white officers or pro gay they were not interested in black case they were there to deny racism it was a racist agenda. So I had 1001 excuses why they could not take on my issue! One of their best excuses was that Race relations no longer existed it was now equal opportunities. So in other words the gays, women, disabled were covered under it but not race! Another classical excuse they loved to use was to find out what area I lived in, and then claimed not to cover that zone! **Expert liars**!

15 January I was told by the community legal advice that Bromford was discriminating against me and that it was clear evidence. **But** they could not take on my case as they could **not** prove where they funds were going too! I had the truth given to me just as long that I could not do anything with it; it seemed that way. Another expert lies and cover up. So here

I was a victim of racial harassment and yet the system claimed they could not prove where the money was going too! In other words the funds were better off not being spent on black people. I hated when an organisation took pleasure in telling me that I was a victim of racism and yet they could do nothing for me. It must be music to their ears!

So I tried more solicitors but was told that if they did practise in that area they no longer did! The law society did **not** seem to update their records as each contact they offered to me only then denied providing that service, or now offered something else! So much for the law always been updated that the student can't keep up!

Other solicitors said that Bromford Housing was racist but it would be civil litigation so I had to pay £150 just for them to look at my papers and that was just for starters and then it depended how long they spent combing through the files and letters past between Bromford and myself. It was back to sniffing dirty knickers again for a few seconds.

Being a poor black man; I could not afford to hire avaricious solicitors to take on a racist Housing Cooperation who had the power and money to fail to attend appointments. So the solicitors admitted there was racism but I had to pay for justice when the **Race Act** was supposed to protect me from both private and public sectors! Bromford could break the law and was doing so and the system allowed them to do it; because it was all a game. The Poor black people could not afford to sue big companies and the government made sure that the single equal opportunity staffs was no longer structured by black people but white faces who seemed to be run by gays and white women out to serve their own marginal groups.

The Race Law and Human Right Act 2000 had become by design to bamboozle black people living in Britain by institutional intention.

25 January according to the South Staffs police Bromford were refusing to take their calls! The crime number given to me they have tried to contact Bromford to tackle the issue but there is a long silence coming from them. Bromford **refuses** to talk to the police! Was this possible? Surely the police had the powers to get Bromford to respond or did they not when it came to racism?

As I listened to the party above and the loud screaming I could not take anymore.

I could not believe that there was a child not going to bed but passively inhaling cannabis and God knows what from her (step father) I later discovered from one of the neighbours. No one complained. Maybe the whole white street was in on the plan to drive this nigger out?

"Bromford emergency out of hours," said the operator.

"There is a party going on and it is loud. My girlfriend can't sleep."

"How long have they been doing this for?" The operator asked.

"All day long! It is getting worse it is now 2:00 am in the morning and I am so tired!"

"I can make a report and file it in the morning," she said. I heard this hundreds of times ringing the office ours throughout January and yet Bromford didn't get back to me.

Chapter Sixteen

February 1st arrived I began to wear headphones all day just to ease the banging upstairs. The noise was so loud that I could pick it up even with head-phones on but it was not bad. But wearing headphones all day was uncomfortable for my ears as they became sore.

No matter how loud the banging and thuds I was not going to respond even if I could hear it through my headphone! They wanted a response from me but they were frustrated as to why I did not respond. I had this horrible hunch that Bromford Housing was involved in this racial harassment but how could I go about proving it? The police could not even get a hold of them to file this charge against the neighbours! Every complaint I made the neighbours countered it with theirs and nothing was ever done. The out of hour's calls was never taken up by Bromford. This now made me realised that I was confident that Bromford Housing Association was behind this racial harassment; but I needed more proof.

I needed Bromford Housing to give out enough rope to hang themselves with; but would they? Would they be so stupid enough that they would slip up and hang themselves using their own rope? Would they set a trap for themselves down the line?

I listened to the police recording on the tape informing me that they were filing my case as they could not get any response from Bromford Housing! My racist neighbours were free to do that they wanted as the police could not get anything from my landlords. So the racists were free because the police claimed that Bromford refused to return their calls!

February 3

I mentally gave in. I could not take anymore. The police was not getting anywhere with Bromford Housing Association there was no contact between either of them. I went to see my doctor looking weak and broken tired and distressed. I needed antidepressants or I was going to kill myself I was so close to it many times. I wanted to die but the only thing that kept me alive was the shock on my girlfriend's face coming home to see my body hanging in mid air my neck broken my eyes popped out their socket. But I really had nothing to live for. England's racist system was breaking me down.

I walked into the medical practice seeing this slim white man sitting there. He was white but not threatening; he had a calm presence about him. I felt safe as if I wanted to be there and never go home to my hell flat. Just one look at me and he knew I was breaking. I didn't feel black just one of his patients. I wished the world was like this but it wasn't.

"What can I do for this?" Doctor Bell asked tenderly.

"I am suicidal. I don't want to live any longer," I almost cried. I told him everything.

"You have been though a lot! The arson attempt on life has only just happened and now this!" I was shocked he still remembered what Cynthia did. I got sleeping pills from him to help me sleep after that incident but was not going to take any other medication associated with mental health. I was so against any kind of drugs.

I just wanted to burst out crying but I knew that like a dam the force of the emotion would not stop and I would be embarrassed. The doctor looked at me he could see that I was going through a lot.

He only had the powers to give me something to help my mental health. Tablets were not going to get rid of racial hate crimes. It was not going to make racist neighbours disappear.

I wondered what they would do for me. I became scared of myself as I was becoming dangerous. I wanted to kill the 'astard to watch the life leave the whites of his very eyes and showing no remorse. The pain Bailey inflicted on me I wanted to return to him but he knew he was invincible. Black lynching was not a thing of the past; it just took on a different shape. White racists were not going to be so blatant about it instead they created mental warfare that was the new century of calling black people niggers without getting into trouble.

"You could see our psychiatrist nurse."

"Would that appear on my record?"

"Yes I am afraid it would."

"I don't want that option," I said sounding faint and exceedingly exhausted.

"Are you sure you are going to be okay?"

I didn't answer.

"I will prescribe you some antidepressants," he said turning to his computer and then writing out the small green prescription.

I was now taking medication for depression. I could not cope with any levels of stress I had such a mental breakdown. I moved into Perton a confident black man but white hate had broken me down where I no longer wanted to live.

Chapter Seventeen

It was now 18 March nothing had changed. Bromford and the police were calling each other liars! Bromford housing Association claimed that the police didn't contact them while the police claimed that they did!

As far as I was concerned they were probably in on the game. I didn't trust the police, and certainly didn't trust Bromford. Another example of institutional racism ran by white people who didn't want to do anything for black victims.

Bailey and I would walk past each other eyeballing while he would call me names. I watched him as he sauntered around like a bouncer showing off yet again another fierce looking fighting bull dog. Now he had two of them and a screaming child living upstairs my flat! I could not believe that Bromford would allow bailey to have two dogs to live upstairs which was against the tenancy agreement. Now I knew it was racial harassment not only from Bailey but Bromford!

"Have you heard anything from the police?" Anne asked me.

I sipped my coffee before answering.

"No."

"Why not?"

"Because the police claimed to have gone around there to find them extra nice," I replied.

"You are kidding me?"

"No Anne. That is what they said." She looked at me disappointingly.

"I am beginning to hate all white people and yet I am dating a white woman!" I said.

"So you're blaming me for everything?"

"No I am just saying that when I look at you I see your white skin; before it was not so noticeable now it just sticks right out."

"I am sorry that I can't relate to you," she said. I was not sure whether she was being genuine or getting back at me.

"No... Only a black woman would know what it is to be black in racist England and this no white woman will ever know or care to even know about," I twisted my words with anger.

I fiddled the remote control just scanning the channels not bothering to even notice what was on television. I sat by the window most of the time just staring into space obsessed with what white person or groups would pull up in their cars. Maybe it would be gangs of them to finally do a Stephen Lawrence on me. I was never safe in Perton not with the police or with Bromford Housing. I now had to live with Bailey speaking in Jamaican patois and being racially offensive towards me.

"So you are going to leave me because I am not black?"

"Did I say that? The thoughts did cross my mind of dating only black women if I am being honest Anne. Someone who understood racism and experienced it there is no other hate that equals to when someone hates you for your skin not being similar to theirs!"

"Do you love me?" She asked.

"Of course I do, it would take more than their evil to stop me loving you," I replied.

"We will then get through it," she tearfully said.

I began to see why so many mixed race children were sent into foster homes being produced by interracial one night stands or weak relationships.

Many white women found it easier to sleep with black men only to then have abortions killing an innocent seed because it was part black than living with the shame of having to walk with their heads low every time they walked past a white bigot.

It was okay for white males to impregnate African and Indian women leaving mulatto children all over the empire but his white women had to deny her these luxuries. There were always double standards where white people were concerned and I was beginning to see it in my personal life.

I looked at Anne. She potentially could be the mother of my children. Could I have children in England whether biracial or black knowing the struggles that they would face? How would Anne cope with her biracial child coming home saying that he or she had experience racism at school? The racism in Britain I was facing in Perton was forcing me to see that having children may be a no go area for me. England was not safe for my children it was not multicultural and it would only get worse no one really cared about the hate that went on unchallenged.

Chapter Eighteen

If things could not get worse they did. Bailey lost his job as a shelf fitter and became increasingly drunk and abusive spending more time winding up his two brute dogs and his step daughter and taking drugs. I at last had the equal opportunity officer at my flat who worked for the Wolverhampton Council.

Her hair was dark her face oval and she was probably in her late fifties. Anne was at work. There was silence upstairs which didn't surprise me as they knew that someone other than Anne was with me.

"My daughter was a victim of racism," she said taking me by surprise. "And she is white." I didn't know what to say it was as if she was playing white magic with my head although I needed her help so was willing to listen to her hogwash. But after I listened to her whinging about her daughter being the so-called victim of racism on closer examination; I realised quickly that it was not because she was white it just happened that the person she was arguing with happened to be black! Now I could see why she had the job of equal opportunity officer; she was well vetted by the council to give black people nothing! Would I be right? Or am I being paranoid? But then why did she tell me about her personal life of her daughter being a victim of so-called racism when there was no logical foundation and it was unethical to discuss personal information? Was she justifying that all is fair in love and war? But since the visit of the equal opportunity officer the noise level could not get any worse!

The child was left alone with two brutes of a dog while her parents went off smoking weed. This was no home for any child to be raised into but Bromford would do anything just to get back at me for talking to the newspapers.

I rang the emergency line and out of hours numerous times and was promised that it would be registered as an ASBO. There was going to be repercussions I thought to myself.

"I will have to leave now," Said Julie the equal opportunity officer after one of her drop in visits. She walked towards the front door when she heard the dog yapping and loud footsteps.

"They obviously think I have gone. That noise is horrendous!" She said.

"That is nothing. That is just them being in a good mood!" I replied.

She made a note of it and left.

It was now **May 5**, Bromford became even more calculating. My complaints were now past over to Julie and not even addressed by their organisation! I could not understand why they would do that when they were the landlords. It was just another racist institutional smokescreen set up as facade to sweep under the carpet intolerance.

My girlfriend and I sat down in our favourite harvester.

"We are going to have to move out," she said finally finishing her elder flower drink.

"When do we start looking for a new home?" I said.

"I will start to look around and asked work colleagues to keep an eye out," she replied.

"It is going to be hard with us having five cats and two guinea pigs. No landlord will touch us," I said wiping away the sticky barbeque ribs from my mouth with a tissue.

"Something has to come up," she said as if my sanity depended on it. "And your doctor is behind the move."

"Everything in England is superficial," I said under my breath. Anne looked at me I could read her mind. I knew what she was thinking but she was wrong.

"They claim to be a nation of animal lovers and yet they don't allow pets."

"Tell me about it," she approved.

"England claims to be everything that she isn't. I never knew that in this modern age in England black people were still forced from their homes," I whispered. "My God it is as if nothing has changed!"

"What do you mean?"

"Well back in the 50s my parent's generation faced the same problem where white people didn't want to have black neighbours sharing the same street so they all moved out. Only this time we are being driven out. It is still the same principle. That was how we had our own Churches as my father told me that when he went to white Churches the white pastors slammed the door in his face. Now there is a black Church the BNP are arguing that blacks are just as racist! It is a game! We have a black police association as the white officers did not cater for ethnic officers and they are called racist!"

"But the whites could not have been proper Christians!" Anne said.

"They would beg to differ," I replied. "The KKK was hard-boiled Baptist who saw no problem lynching black men while worshipping Jesus!"

Anne was quiet for a while. It was as if she didn't know that there were white Christians who murdered black people. It was too much for her judging by her facial expression.

"We are going to have to move out quickly. What about the race organisations can't they find us a place to live?" She asked.

"Anne..." I breathed in despair, "I contacted around all their organisations but they either tell me that I am not living in their area or come up with some other outlandish reasons why they can't deal with my situation. I am hitting my head against a brick wall."

"So why are they there for?" She asked. Her question forced me to laughter.

"I looked at one of human right sites and who were they defending? But a white polish man discriminated by another white English person. That is how they get around it. It's a game to them! And here we are being forced to move of our homes. You know what it worse Anne?"

"What?"

"The racist system is so cunning that they would rather use your white face and call you the victim rather than use mine! And if I objected they would call me a racist! Any wonder why black people don't report racism as they know it will do no good. Every other group benefit from our cause and yet who's been hurt the most in history and still do today?"

"Don't worry we will move out."

I was not happy with those words.

"Whatever."

"Are most whites racists I mean minority groups like gays?"

"What! I know from experience," I screamed out loudly, "I and a friend of mine used to go to gay nightclubs thinking there would be no racism... but they are worse than any other so-called oppressed minority group! They refuse to talk to you unless they want to bed you!"

"What about the deaf community have you experience racism from them?"
"I don't know why but no! Even back in the racist 80s I encountered white deaf people but I have never felt hatred or cold gaze coming from them. That is so strange. They must go through some real shit," I whispered almost trying to figure it out.
It was England way past the millennium, streets party and social changes technology advancement, science figuring out space and open heart surgery with laser operation, but yet a black man was forced out from his house.
I might as well be shipped from Africa after my parents had rebuild England and made her what she is today. I was just attacked from a subtle but vicious angle. There was not one public body that offered me advice regarding my human rights to be safe in my own home.
Any public body that got involved in my case but only for a fleeting moment the acting solicitors always ended up leaving and my files lost! Or they failed to turn up to any meetings arranged with myself and Bromford. And this happened time and time again... I would end up with weedy and pale looking solicitors who looked as if they had just risen from the grave; lacking energy, and never did last to complete the project.
So I was failed left right and centre by the system that had their own agenda to make sure that the race laws remained redundant, and the black voice or pain is never heard. The local council who funded these public bodies would suddenly cut their funding anytime the black race card reared her ugly head, and causing trouble organisations to be left without jobs.

It was therefore easier for council workers to remain employed, and not on the dole; but dealing with sex and gender orientation or overweight ginger-headed discrimination no matter how trivial. I was sure that within the system anyone showing an interest in race were either victimised or lost their jobs it didn't make any sense why I could not get any help from anyone. Or maybe it was organised and cleverly maintained by a group of white racists?

May 26

I spent 12 hours at the steam room! The regulars who went there were shocked that I was there for so long and even made comments but I said nothing. I just could not bring myself to go home. The noise had become worse. There was nothing that I could do. Every complaint I gave to Bromford they would pass it on to Julie and nothing got done. It was the usual turn a blind eye to race no one cared or even wanted to break a sweat. My black pain was not worth white effort. I sat in the boiling steam room sapping every depression from both mind and body. I could not cope.

I really didn't want to live anymore. The only thing that kept me alive was my girlfriend. Racism in England had driven me to the feelings of wanting to take my own life. I would want to drive into a brick wall and just see my blood all over the walls my black brains for the white racist to see what they have done yet again to another nigger. Their cruelty was the same whether it was sticking a knife into an innocent black man or victimizing him into taking his own life.

I grew to hate my black skin, and the pain it created for me. It became so heavy almost like black bin liners carrying rubbish for people to dump their racist garbage into. Everywhere I went. I could not breathe in the fresh air or even admire the morning dew across the country fields because I aware I was a nigger and niggers were not suppose to behave in a certain way but to enjoy nigger music.

I could not shop without being followed or watched by security staff paid to stereotype every black male that enters any shop. Their eyes would follow you like vultures stalking their prey waiting to pounce and make that arrest. I only had to look into a shopping window and white women would jump out of their skin seeing a black face looking in; or if I suddenly walked up behind them the street it was enough for them to hold on to their handbags.

The nights were worse. If ever I wanted to believe that I was a black rapist was at night I only had to walk the streets. The fear on white women's faces when a black man was walking even on opposite the side of the street... nowhere near her was evident to see. It hurt deeply. White people define who I was how I behaved and what pain they could inflict upon me. It was only fighting that I could get any justice as hardly any white people in England really cared about black people or even wanted us to have justice in their court rooms. I didn't trust white people any longer only the small friends around me. Whenever I walk or did any shopping I avoided why people their racist gaze their hate I could feel the intensity of their disgust that they had for black people. But their victimised us in a worse way mentally. They gave us bad customer services or created noises from hell anything to break down the black race.

The neighbour's dogs were fully grown and this just added to the sheer weight of hell. I could not spend any time in the home that I was paying Bromford rent too. The thought of suicide was never far from mind. I became afraid of living and dying tasted like freedom. England was the black man's hell enticed to our parents that if we fought their dirty wars against the Germans... clean up their filthy streets and work in their dark and derelict factories; we would be accepted but it was lies. No English child today knew that black people died in both wars fighting for Britain. The school would rather teach gay sex!
Black people honoured the queen more than the English; we had all Lady Diana's wedding photos; the queen's jubilee plates and still when we tried to live next door to white people they moved out. They simply wanted to nothing to do with black people and their laws and their system showed it.
I didn't want to be tried to be liked by white people anymore. I didn't care about them. I was not going to try hard anymore. I was tired of integrating speaking the Queen's good English but yet still I was a nigger. The only good nigger that white people liked was those in the ghettos living on hand-outs or better still those who left the country. I hated the system and became the hate that hate created. I hated England every green grass in it. I didn't want to be a Martin Luther King or Malcolm X but the strong black panthers or nation of Islam.

So I began watching videos of black empowerment to try to learn to love myself again. White people wanted me to hate me. I had to fight back. I watched videos of Louise Farrakhan and his message to black people who lived in a white world that will never accept us. It all made sense to me.

At times I wanted to leave my Christian faith and I no longer practised it. I couldn't. Christianity was brought into Africa under false pretences like my parents were encouraged into England to be nannies to white babies the same who would grow up and call them niggers. Christianity was not working for me. It was not revolutionary; it was all about heaven... while living in a white man's hell on earth.

I have prayed and prayed until my tears became drops of blood and yet no white God answered me. Something had to be wrong with the faith that was given to my ancestors. While I read my bible devotedly seeking first the kingdom of heaven white people didn't have to do that. While I was told to be faithful to God; white people didn't have to that. Black people were taught to suffer for the kingdom of heaven sake while having the Churches burnt down God never did intervene. The number of black children who lost their lives when white people burnt down their Churches made me questioned my faith now. All these things now bothered me. I became preoccupied with race and became fill with so much hate that it was making me angry and ill. I could not understand how white people could not be ill by the hate their carried around with them to even teaching their babies to hate.

I began to feel ill as I hated white people so much now. Believing in Jesus; I was told to turn the other cheek and during slavery that was just what we did and continued doing.

I didn't want to love my enemies so I could not be a good Christian. I didn't want to love white people who plotted to burn my flat down or drive me into insanity or even loved a racist institution. Such logic was absurd.

No wonder black people were weak and never fought back only against each other. How could you love a race who hated you since history to plot genocide against your race? Does the Jews love the Germans, or the Chinese the Japanese; or Vietnamese the Americans?

I wanted to be the spirit of Martin Luther King's dream not noticing the colour of white people's skin but it was impossible now. For every good one white person that I saw there that were thousands that was bad. Hate was unnatural to me and yet white people found it easy to hate black people. Where did they hate come from? Hate was not being human it was dark anger and irrational. It was Hitler's hate this anger which gassed millions of Jews and wanting to create the super white race. He had no problem killing babies as so do the KKK this kind of hate I did not want and yet I wondered if I was capable now of watching a white person dying without even flinching? But then again I had a neighbour that was a capable of watching me reach breaking point showing no mercy with one aim only to drive me out of my home. I hated him in self defence, but he hated me simply because he was racist.

Chapter Nineteen

It was a hot summer days in May 20 when my white friend and I were working on our bicycles. We shared a bit of laughter between us trying to pump up the bicycle only for it to fall against his car.

"You're clumsy Jonathon!" I laughed.

"You know I have awkward coordination."

"I am looking for a good cycle," I said getting a thrill watching him struggle with the easy task of pumping up the wheel.

Out of nowhere Bailey strolled over toward us with his two big ugly looking dogs offering me out.

"You think you're tough then?" He challenged feeling confident that his two dogs wanted black blood. I looked at the dogs not wanting to provoke him or them. Every white person knew that black people hated dogs it had something to do with police setting dogs onto black people doing civil rights and it was something that stuck ever since.

"Come on then!" He continued his provocation.

"You start first," I said still scared of the dogs. I knew one bite from those dogs in the right place and I was dead black meat. It quickly turned into fiery confrontations of words.

"Stop it at once!" My friend shouted his face bright red. "You are causing an affray!" As if by white magic those words did the tricks. Bailey quickly walked away with his dogs. I would be mad to try and take him on with his two brute of a dog and a police force that never remained impartial where black people were concerned. I was not going to fall for his trap.

From then every time I left my flat; Bailey also left accompanied by his two big dogs which my friend noticed much to his distress.

My friend and I were both in the garden.

"Look Jonathon; Bailey wants to fight me again!" My friend wouldn't look as he hated any kind of stress.

"Look he is standing there with his dogs offering me out!" But still he refused to look.

May 21 I sat at my flat explaining to a blonde rounded face police woman about the incident. She just stared at me chewing gum which was irritating as her mouth would make all those horrible slushy noises as she chewed. Her eyes were dark gothic distant not caring just chewing loudly almost looking like someone who lacked culture and good breeding.

"I am sorry Kevin but there is nothing on record about your complaint," she said. I was shocked it didn't add him. Why did she then mention about the car park racist incident? How come she knew that I was having problems in the past with the neighbours?" Something smelt fishy. The police force or this police woman was being dishonest. The police yet again was showing that when it came to racism they didn't give a damn. Here was a white police woman a minority group because of her gender yet had the power to inflict injustice on black victims!

22 May

My white friend and I made a statement to the police regarding the neighbours.

"If you spend less time at home that would be good," said the police officer.

"I intend too!" I replied.

"You said you are moving out?"

"Yes."

"We will arrest him then but only after you have left the flat." I agreed to stay away from my own safety! I could not believe that the system who swore by law to protect victims was telling a black man to not spend time in his own flat! It became a joke. How did I know they were going to arrest Bailey? How many more lies were they going to tell me? Maybe they just wanted me out of the way and it was all a con?

I didn't trust anything white people had to say anymore. If the judiciary system could cover up white people murdering black people then the laws had more values protecting cats and dogs than it did niggers. Somehow I had a gut feeling that it was going to be another white lie

Bromford landlord finalise the agreement of my moving home after my doctor's letter sent to them. We started to gather boxes. I could not believe that I was moving out. But the pain would forever be there. I was wounded inside my heart and my soul. White hate had left their prints inside of me. I had changed as a person. My bruised body felt faint; I had lost a sense of self. It was as if I had been buried inside a cold coffin dead to the world but now to be awakened from this death dream. But would I ever feel again? Would I ever laugh or smile like I used too or have the powers of white racism took something away from deep inside of me?

Bromford told me that they told the neighbours that I was moving out within a few days; but they became worse. I never knew white people could hate so deeply without having a conscience to even giving me a few days of peace and silence.

My flesh was torn and dangling from a tree swinging high with spears being pushed into my bruised body. Despite Bromford breaking confidentiality act by sharing information that I was leaving, their vulture and carnal nature lust for further black blood continued unrestraint. Now I realised why there were Black and Asian neighbourhoods in Britain where in these grubby ghettos no one dared leave their houses to venture out for the greener grass as to do so was suicide. England was segregated by race and this was created by hate and this hate was created as they simply don't want black people on their soil... most white people!

Although I hardly eat out now; I always have guessing games with myself to see how long a white people sitting with their families would stare at me for and how long for without removing their gaze. I would predict that as soon as I walk into any room how the floorboards would creak and conversations would suddenly come to a halt with all eyes menacingly questioning what was a nigger doing in their part of the world.

As a black man in Britain I did not have any true peace and happiness in my own life or at home. I could leave my house because in black areas I could be mistaken for a rival gang member and shot at as happened so many times. If I lived in the most deprived ghetto areas filled with emptiness and crack smokers hustling me for money after I just paid for my groceries then I had no dreams only seeing ethnic faces unemployed or gossiping in corner barber shops.

The streets were filthy the atmosphere hopeless where everyone was either hustling trying to make a bit of money because all we had were seasonal Christmas jobs only to be laid off when whites no longer wanted black workers.

I opted from living in the ghetto because I thought England was paved with gold and I wanted to chase some of it but I only moved into a web of deceit and cruel segregation. My dreams were shattered. If I thought England was heaven; I was wrong. If I thought England taught Christian values and respected all faiths I was wrong. It was all a slimy veneer. Everyone's faith was respected just as long as we remained in our little ghettos shooting at each other destroying our own neighbourhoods.

I wore dark glasses so that white people did not see the white pupils of my eyes. They might see my black skin but they would never see my soul which mirrored through my eyes. They would never see if they were hurting me as the dark shades shielded my soul from being penetrated. I never used to wear dark specs before until I moved to Perton but now whenever I leave my home they were on my face. I could not walk around England without these dark shades as whatever they do to me they don't know how I am reacting as they could not see the hurt in my eyes.

They could not see the sadness, the hurts, or the pain as all they saw was a` fashionable black man who thought listened to gangster rap and reggae all day and night. They would like to see my emotions but I would not allow it. If my eyes were hurting it did not show behind the dark tints.

Chapter Twenty

My Freedom at Last!

There was a letter on the floor from Bromford. They had told the neighbours about the noise they were making on the day I was moving out! Bromford timed it so well that it just added salt to injury. I was so deeply hurt that Bromford could play this game right to the very end where they pretend to act against racism but of course when I had already been driven out off my home!

But anyway I would be going despite the nasty and deceitful blow they had delivered. I could almost see the grinning smile on their face as they posted that letter knowing that both their and the white neighbours understood the joke! White hate had won, as they got rid of the nigger from the neighbourhood. For Going to the Voice Newspaper; Bromford was going to teach me a lesson. And they did!

But like Moses leading the children of Israel to the promise land away from slavery; I was moving out of Perton! My friends and my girlfriend's work mates working carrying boxes under the intense heat while curtain were twitching. The white neighbours all came out laughing and whispering to each other but I just wanted to get out.

We all created a line making it easier to move out the things quicker into the waiting vans. I couldn't bring myself to look at the neighbours all outside finding it amusing even the old white lady who gossiped about the local dealer who she claimed sold illegal drugs. But now they were all united glad to see the back of this nigger despite I did no wrong! I could not believe how bare faced and two face they were.

While some of them pretended to be nice to my face their true colours were shown when I was moving out. **White united front** it could not be helped and with chorus from Elgar Land of Hope and Glory with Blake's Jerusalem it was no wonder that England struggled to come to terms with having black neighbours.

I moved into my new four bedroom cottage with two bathrooms and a large lounge and dining room.

"Sorry you can't move in just yet," my landlord said. We all left the furniture in the van and cars.

"Why?" I asked my knees buckling now with fear.

"Bromford said that there was a police incident which involved you," he said grimed face as if he was talking to a crook who tried to deceive him.

"Yes... I called the police as I was the victim! Bromford knows that!"

"They never said that!" He scowled.

"What happening now?" My girlfriend asked.

"We can't move in!" I said. Shit now I was going to be homeless I thought.

"I am going to have to ask for a £500 deposit," the landlord said.

"Oh my God," I said remembering how Bromford promised my doctors that they were behind the move.

"£500?!" Anne exclaimed.

We did not budget for that so it took us by horror. I watched the vans and cars not knowing what to do. I was now homeless with nowhere to go. My freedom from Bromford was going to cost me blood.

"I will lend you the money," Jonathon said.

As if those were the magic words we were given the go ahead to move in.

The cottage was two knocked into one so it was really big. The lounge was enormous and the dining room impressive. I even had an office. Despite the sheer beauty I was sore inside. I just wanted peace and silence no music no nothing just to not hear a pin drop. That was what my spirit craved more than size of a house just to be able to live in peace and without harassment for being the wrong colour.

3 June

I returned to Auden View Perton to clean up the flat. It was one of the worse things that I could have done. I was shocked when we arrived back there. The sun was smiling almost flirting with me. There were fresh flowers on all the neighbour's doors, with even brown hanging baskets! Grubby growling unshaven Bailey even spit polished his front door until he could see his own reflection, to even moving ASDA trolley which he always kept on the path to prevent me from crossing into my own path! He must have been proud getting rid of a nigger.

The place was sparkling as if God had walked through the place. Whiteness had restored black to England's green and pleasant land the land of their high hope and God's radiant glory.

Now I knew what Elgar's, and Blake's stirring and patriotic music and lyrics really meant when it reached its crescendo singing about England's green and pleasant land bringing many whites to their knees as if overcome by the possibility of having all darkies doing an exodus. I could see Blake's lyrics as I looked around Perton.

Black people were not really wanted around white towns where the Church bell faithfully would ring out and Sunday mornings with the smell of roast pork was cooking in the oven.

The neighbours had built their own white Jerusalem now that the satanic mills which were not about Dickens' London work houses but black skin had been dealt with and where white victory had once again rule the waves with fortitude.

They had fought against black evil, resisted black presence, with their bow of burning desire, and with their sharp spears, and with their clashing swords wielding over their heads they delivered their last final blow until they had established in Perton the England that they wanted to see. They finally got rid of the nigger. If they could do it to me then it sent out clear signals from the mountain top to other white people that in the end evil always win.

Because they don't want their little white lily princess playing with nigger boys, or girls building sandcastles on the yellow sandy beach; or walking to school together as it might give their daughters ideas about intermarriage. England was not multicultural this was all a myth I thought as I weakly looked around.

I walked inside the float; but I became more faintish... now I could not breathe. I was having a panic attack. I began to realise that the hell I had been through had affected mentally more that I had realised. Something medically was wrong with me now. I could feel it I just didn't know what yet.

"I will clean," my girlfriend said as I looked as if I was going to pass out. The walls seem to understand my pain, and the pale white ceiling looked as if they were going to drip blood on me.

I could not breathe; I could feel the heat of the arson attempt on my life; I could hear the noises; the racial threats the denial of justice; police lies, and Bromford victimisation. It was as if there was a black hole inside the flat and that black hole was me. There was a lot of pain that I could not describe. It was as if I had just been told that someone close to me had died. I was broken and inwardly bruised.

"Sorry I can't seem to feel my body," I whispered. I looked at my white girlfriend.

Her skin was white, but she stuck with me through it all no matter what. She was my white angel. There she was mopping up my pain; my blood; my grief splashed against with such force against the flat walls.

As I watched her cleaning the room it was as if the flat became my body; I had lost so much identity. The experience was strange going back there. It was as if the flat absorbed so much of my pain and feelings of suicide. Did the flat become me? Did it absorb me in some way? Then why did the walls look as if they were bleeding and the ceiling looked as if they had been brutalised? Could walls really listen? I looked at the big hole, Anne was patching up; in the bathroom door where I had punched it out with my fist imagining it to be Bailey's face. The hole in the door brought back the memories on how I was provoked into insanity and enrage. I never threw my fist into any walls or doors before and I was shocked that I was capable of that amount of damage.

Anne was cleaning up my body so that I could live again; breathe again feel again. There had been many times when I attacked her verbally for being white for not understanding black pain but she stood by my side. That was going to be the woman that I marry.

We had been through so much she could have walked out on me but she stuck it out. Not even racism was going to ruin my relationship with her.

*

Once I settled into our new cottage with my girlfriend who I was now engaged to; the police did not chase up arresting Bailey as they promised, or charging him for anything! It was as if they just wanted us out of the way so they could scrap the whole matter! I had suffered severe racial harassment and threats but yet there was yet again another cover up.

'Julie' who worked for Dudley Council Equal opportunity the now Single Equal opportunity claimed that there was nothing she could do about Bromford racism towards me as I had now moved into a different country like 20 miles away! She eventually left working there! It was almost as if everything was well timed where Council funded bodies knew how to play the system. The signal they gave out to the likes of Bailey was that: you can drive a nigger out off his home as the system will never bring them to justice for it. The local council had every loop hole in the books as to how they could prevent giving black people who had suffered racism, justice. They had every reason as to why cases had to be closed or filed.

And this was because crime against black people in England was not treated as real lawbreaking, but minor offence; if that. Blacks people were not under the Queen's peace; but seen as aliens who were not wanted here to begin with. We were second class citizens; an ethnic minority meaning heathen, pagan, and immigrants not wanted not being a part off.

I thought about all of this in my new garden next to a small running pond with a mini waterfall; the rich sound is like angel music and spirit healing. It was as if nature was healing my mind and body telling me everything will be okay. I sat and listened to the water it being soft and enticing not sadistic and hostile. I had changed. I was a changed man. They say when you have your heart broken in love it will never be the same no matter how you move on to the next love.

Life had broken me. As a baby I was not black when I first learnt to speak I was not black; I was pure. Now living in white Britain I wanted to question why was I born a black baby. Why could I not have been born white not knowing what real pain is? Why did black people have to suffer more than anyone else? And why did the British government invited my parents to England in the first place knowing that this would lead to nothing more than our victimisation; once we had cleaned up England after the wars they had with Germany? Because: we fought on the side of the British; shed blood for the English, marched faithfully in their trenches; but now they did not want us here.

England was no longer my home. So my blood could not rest on English soil; my ashes had to scattered where hate did not exist, and where the beat of the African drums enticed my spirit back to the motherland. Where; my spirit soar the African paradise; free from white racism inhaling freedom knowing happiness and celebrating blackness without shame.

Chapter Twenty One

The Battle for Justice

As for Bromford: I could not take my case to court, as the courts would not touch it unless I had exhausted the complaint procedure. This became Bromford's grenades in which they kept hurling at me until they wore me down into the ground.

Bromford would not budge on moving forward with my grievance. This became their ace card which they kept playing knowing that soon the statute of limitation would kick in!

In the end the case was now three years old so nothing could be done because of **statute** of **limitation** even though a crime has been committed which was institutional racism as defined by the McPherson report! You could molest a woman, whether fifty years ago or not; and this statute of limitation would not invalid her claim for justice as it would be seen as a criminal offence against a person. Racism against black people was not seen as a criminal offence as you had to have forwarded your complaint within a given time the rules changes where women are concerned.

However, I even sent a cheque to Bromford offices for them to release my files under the **freedom** of **information act**, but to this day they had not released my papers despite proof that Bromford had cashed the cheque as confirmed by my bank! Bromford first denied that I sent them a cheque but when pressed into the corner with evidence; they then retracted, and claimed to have lost it! But it was cashed!

Another game used by racist institutions trying to cover their own back is to claim to have lost your files, 'an honest accident' Bromford and I battled for a while corresponding by letter but they still would not release my files despite the bank showing that they had in fact cashed my cheque made payable to Bromford only.

It took Bromford three months to reply to a letter which they claimed would take seven-fourteen days! A quarter of a year! They played the game very well knowing that time would be eventually on their side. The English courts must have known that this was a legal loophole?

Cheshire, Halton & Warrington Race & Equality Centre was interested in the case but warned that they were not funded for racism any longer despite being called race and Equal Centre! So I had to pay a percentage if they took on the case and won. Naturally I agreed. However, they sent me an email to tell me that they now progressed to dealing with employment cases only and was unable to assist me further! Why did this not surprise me?

Chapter Twenty Two

By keeping a daily record of my experiences, letters from Bromford, correspondence, and now turning it into a short novel; it has kept me from ultimately taking my own life. It became my emotional punch bag when at times I wanted to run up to a white person who after giving me racist glares and putting a fist in their faces.

Because: the white racist system had created a hate machine; a ticking time bomb where I wanted justice for what had happened to me. By their silence, and inaction the system had told me that black life had no value.

The rage in me became the inferno of hate where if a white person looked at me I just wanted to fight them even if it meant being locked up. I was an angry black man on the loose vowing that whites would not hurt me again.

Where Christianity was concerned: I had lost my faith. I no longer practised it, as I could not attend a Church singing, and shouting praises to a God when he had allowed me to go through so much racial abuse and not intervened. But should God have intervened? Should he have answered my prayers when so many times at Perton I was on my knees praying for peace?

There were times when the tears were falling like drops of blood my asking God for him to remove away the racist neighbours. But I would open my eyes waiting to see if I could walk out the door and like Moses seeing the back of God witnessing a dramatic change. It would only become worse.

I used to listen to black preachers incoherently ranting and raving about Jesus turning water into wine, healing the sick, yet here I was on medication diagnosed with bipolar by psychiatrists in Telford, because of white hate.

I read the professor: Richard Darkin's book: 'The God delusion' just trying to make sense of my life and whether I had to live with racism, and forget a world that was made by a loving God as it didn't make sense to me. A God who loved would not have made a human being go through this amount of pain and ignored their prayers.

Atheism began to appeal to me as time went on. At least as an atheist you learnt to live with evil and not try to rationalise why human beings were so evil.

I did not believe that horses and Christ riding on it was going to come charging from the skies as I was previously taught. Racism had knocked out that romantic sentiment and innocence of believing in religion of believing in a God who loved and cared for us.

God could not be a God of love, and yet the Church was still struggling with racism. Maybe human beings were just horrible and products of evolution; coming from nothing, and going to nothing? Where was this love; if God was love? There were no reasons for me to be in Church any longer.

Of course I had a hole inside of me; but reason was stronger than fantasy. The romantic sentiment I had of believing in religion and in a God who turned water into wine; had been sucked out of my soul; leaving behind just anger.

I was now sick suffering from clinical depression, and social anxiety where at any moment I could ape out against white hate. Before I could have handle racism, by ignoring it, even if it was in my face; like so many black people have learnt to do; but now I had no internal mechanism for it.

I could not even turn a blind eye to it as so many black people do every day. I had to react to any, and everything. I had to try, and avoid looking into white people's eyes and seeing their hatred as this would only wind me up. So I would sometimes cross the street just to avoid contact with white people. I became a mental mess and without my faith in a fantasy God I had no release.

The black Churches functioned on dance, and good music, dancing away the trials of everyday racism that they experienced in white England. But this was no longer a release for me. As when I looked up at the skies; I didn't see a Jesus on his white horse waving his sword against my enemies; but clouds. I moved to Perton believing in miracles; believing in hope and human potential to love but now I had given up on all that. England was cold, cruel and racist.

The Jesus in me had been beaten out as I was no longer interested in turning the other cheek. I was not going to give my cloak, and my staff, and walk that extra mile as my pastor taught for any white racist. Living in England without a faith in God was going to be challenging. It was unusual as faith was what kept black people sane during slavery. But what did God do for me?

The slightest of noise to this day of my cats running up stairs even against softened carpets got me shaking. I was so damaged by the noise pollution the neighbours had made that my friends had to encourage me to say that it was over I was in a new place with wonderful landlords.

Chapter Twenty Three

"You really had suffered haven't you?" The Indian female counsellor said to me after I revealed what had happened to me from the arson attempt to constant racial harassment. She was only a small woman. Her hair jet black tied into a ponytail. She was not black; but I felt safe with her like I did Doctor Bell.

"How has this affected you Kevin?" She continued.

"I hate white peoples," I barked my chest feeling hate.

"Are you saying all white people are racist?"

"Most of them are unless you could prove from you own experience that they are not?"

She was quiet as if reflecting on her own experience.

"How do you move forward?" She asked me.

"You're the counsellor," I said, "you tell me." She sweetly smiled.

"You have a lot of anger in you Kevin."

"I was not born with anger or hate," I fired back; "society made me that way! You can't go on loving your enemies forever who tries to hurt you!"

"But the great leader Martin Luther King taught love," she said thinking that by mentioning his name it would put the world to right between black and whites.

"And where did that get him in the end? What people don't tell you is that towards the end of his life; he realised that a passive approach was no longer effective."

She talked about Martin Luther King and Malcolm X it was a nice feeling listening to this Indian woman who could connect with my history without a condescending manner or for sinister benefit such as to water me down.

I would meet her on a regular basis and it was good just talking to her and getting things off my chest. She could relate. She was not white; it was that simple.

I was so angry that on a number of occasions the counselling session would be interrupted by concerned staff opening the door, thinking that my counsellor was being attacked physically by me! Of course once the staff got to know me they realised that I was just an angry black man who had experienced some crap in my life.

But on our next meeting I was hit with bad news. This Indian counsellor sat at the table eyes fastened to mine. I was sure that if I was not with Anne; I would have dated this Indian woman or or go back to dating my own race. It was not that I was against interracial dating but in England it was hard work. Naturally, during times of racial injustice, and experiencing pain; I found difficulty embracing what reminded me of the world.

"You need to have psychotherapy counselling for trauma and I am not qualified in that area," she said.

"Your skin makes you qualified," I said angrily. She laughed. Maybe she agreed with me.

"You will be seen by a specialist..."

..."White person," I interrupted?"

"Don't judge until you see them," she said.

When she said that: I thought of Doctor Bell; the sweetest professional white man any black person could ever have met. It was a shame most white people were not like him I thought to myself.

"I had a good doctor who was a white man," I said to her at last breaking the silence. She embraced herself as if waiting for bad news.

"And what happened or what did he do?"

"He could not do enough! He was gentle, understanding I didn't even notice his skin colour. The world should be like that. If he voted for the far right it would not bother me as he was professional in his job! He wrote to Bromford telling them that I had to move out as I was going through racial harassment." Those words surprised her. It was as if she did not see them coming. I continued to shock her. "In the end we all have the same blood; the same shape. When I am with my friends, I don't see colour, but human beings. Where did it all go wrong? We can fly to the moon and back, and yet with that same skill, we kill, and commit human genocide! When I play the piano I have so much love for everyone no matter what colour. Sometimes I am like a child just born that what music does to me. I don't notice races or colour. But when I leave my home, and the safety of it; the evil in the world just hit me. You feel it from people; their eyes and cold stares, and so you conform to this energy it is all out there evil... no love just racial hate towards black people!"

She was quiet just staring lovingly at me.

"Well the white people who love you they can share this love, but the others it is their loss," she said choking back emotions but disguising it behind a cough.

Chapter Twenty Four

Now I attended intensive trauma counselling, but this time looking into the deep blue eyes of a white female psychotherapist trying to remove the word racism from my experience.

Here she was trying to so-called heal me, and my pain, but yet I could not used the very word that was at the heart of my experience.

It was like telling a Jew not to use the word holocaust! In the end I realised that the counselling was just making me angrier, and all about making white people look good for the damage they had caused black people.

In the end I preferred the Indian female counsellor who could relate to me, but had her hands tied. My pain could only be healed by a non-white and yet most therapists were white people! Would a woman be happy being counselled by a man if she was raped? Or Jews not mind being counselled by Germans over the holocaust?

In the end I struggled with the idea of sitting with white counsellors revealing that white people don't want black people living in England. It just did not made any sense. But in the end black people were used to having white people sit on race relations employed by the local council to frustrate black social economic progress.

So the black experience became like George Orwell's 1984 nightmare where words didn't mean what they suppose to anymore. Everything was true, with the exception of course racism.

The gays, and the Jews, disabled, and women could define their pain; but racism was only a concept that was a figment of the black mind, which could be narrowed down to a medical condition... schizophrenia. And that was how white people saw black people who had been a victim or white hate. But we either learn to live with racism; and don't talk about it, or are seen as trouble makers or worse schizophrenic.

Or we end up meeting with our racist neighbours over a cup of tea, and a bit of green salad and English scone; observed by a simple-faced advocate was another option. Because it was never racism a black person is told under this George Orwell 1984 England, that we experienced; but character difference or misunderstanding! But no gay person yet had ever been called schizophrenic for his pain or women for theirs or having character differences or misunderstandings!

But then the system was run by white heterosexual males, gays, lesbians, white women, disabled, Scots, Irish; all claiming to be a minority group but all still have one thing in common: **white power**!

The psychiatrists were trying to sort out my medication for two years as the quetiapine also known as seroquel would knock me out for 24 hours leaving me sedated. My mind was not functioning at all. My speech was slurry, and I moved around like a lifeless zombie not knowing what day or time it was. I just slept and slept and ate nothing more.

My body was ultra sensitive to any medication so they had to find the right ones which worked for me. So I was just popping back pills until the right ones worked for me.

I could not cope without my medication they helped controlled my rage my inner anger. The pills became what the Holy Ghost was to black people; the comforter.

If I tried to go without them I soon realised that my mental state just declined. Racism did that to me. It damaged me socially where I would not perform live any longer. My friends had problems getting me to socialise or to go into certain places. I had been damaged. Since being in Telford I have met some new white friends from both males and females but time would have to be a great. There are good white people out there; but sadly they are hard to find in an England where the media rather divide, and conquer, to spread propaganda. That is what constructs racial conflicts and hatred. The media, and those who would rather spread hate, and a strategic government who snub teaching white children the significance of why black people came into this country to begin with. That information would solve a lot of hate crimes but would it be in the government interest for poor whites and blacks to come together? Is that what their really want?

My only light at the end of the tunnel was writing this book and letting everyone know what I had suffered under Bromford Housing Association and how it had affected my mental health where I could be taking medication for the rest of my life because they didn't want us here!

I would forever keep my files and correspondence between Bromford and myself and records just as a reminder that most white people (not all) don't want niggers for a neighbour.

I would never be at peace until justice against Bromford has been served, or everyone knew the pain and how institutional racism was still rampant despite the veneer of the British claiming that moves were made in which to tackle it head on!

Copies of this book I will send to:

Charities Commission
The Voice Newspaper
The Guardian
Jamaican cleaner
Housing Ombudsman etc...
Socialist Worker

Bromford's list of failures and breaches of my Human Right 2000: (ECHRA 2010 known today since time of publication)

1. Intentional infliction of emotional distress.

2. Failure in their duty of care.

3. Hate crimes which are reported should be responded to within 48hrs by law. Bromford did not respond at all to any of my complaint regarding racial harassment.

4. Article 8 everyone has a right to be safe within their property.

5. Everyone has a right to live without being discriminated against in conjunction with article 8 of the HRA.

July 2003. The local authority had powers to prevent or impose sanctions on racist behaviours and yet I lost my home as a result!

6. Everyone has a right under freedom of information to get access to their files. Bromford cashed my cheque and denied my basic human rights claiming to have lost this cheque despite it being cashed by their own hands according to my bank.

6. Under extreme circumstances I had suffered ill health and was forced to move.

7. Intentional harassment.

8. Bromford gave misinformation to my landlord and neighbours thus breaking the confidential act.

9. Bromford was in breach of their own tenancy agreement in which to protect their tenants from noise pollution.

Dedication

This book I dedicate to all my genuine white friends, and white family, both personally and on Face Book who have tried to make the worlds a better and equal place for us all to live in and for those who have the ability to see beyond the colour of man's skin.

The book has been written dealing with raw emotion showing real pain, and anger at the time of writing; and therefore I would not do it justice if it was edited. But this book is not directed against those whites whom I deeply love and cherish, but it is against those whites who have power sitting in local government, institutions and private sectors who have created a social condition which helps generate the ugly face of racism.

This book is also dedicated to the memory of Michael Schwerner, aged 24, Andrew Goodman, 20, both from New York and James Chaney, 22, from Meridian, Mississippi.

These two white guys; with their black friend, were assassinated by the KKK for refusing to party to white hate! In the face of death these two white guys could have saved their own lives, but chose to die like men. And men in deed they are! These two white **heroes;** I salute with the utter respect. (Mississippi Burning film)

http://news.bbc.co.uk/onthisday/hi/dates/stories/august/4/newsid_29 62000/2962638.stm

Printed in Great Britain
by Amazon.co.uk, Ltd.,
Marston Gate.